'García Robayo write
and a fai
T

'There are very few writers who can challenge expectations the way García Robayo does. She is simply one of the best of the new generation that respects, yet no longer identifies with, the Latin American Boom.'
Mariana Enríquez

'García Robayo's voice is a scalpel cutting into – with fine and precise incisions – the flesh of our personal life.'
Juan Gabriel Vásquez

'One of the most potent figures of contemporary Latin American literature.'
ABC CULTURAL

'García Robayo doesn't pretend to be good or docile or seductive and yet, paradoxically, the complexity of her thinking manifests itself in a style that is kind. Hers is a kindness that thrives on discomfort: the contradiction of a great novelist.'
Alejandro Zambra

'García Robayo is building one of the most solid and interesting oeuvres in Latin American literature.'
Juan Cárdenas

'Margarita shows sharp insight into contemporary life. Her voice speaks with surreptitious irony and sophisticated psychological perception. She is the creator of an exceptional poetics of displacement.'
Juan Villoro

THE DELIVERY

First published by Charco Press 2023
Charco Press Ltd., Office 59, 44-46 Morningside Road, Edinburgh
EH10 4BF

A CIP catalogue record for this book is available
from the British Library.

ISBN: 9781913867690
e-book: 9781913867706

www.charcopress.com

Edited by Fionn Petch
Cover designed by Pablo Font
Typeset by Laura Jones
Proofread by Fiona Mackintosh

Margarita García Robayo

THE DELIVERY

Translated by
Megan McDowell

CHARCO PRESS

To Vicente and Julieta, my home.

First it was like the intrusion of a fly in wintertime.
Such a strange thing. The eyes follow its flight.
The ear tries to catch its buzzing.
The fly lands on the table
on the light bulb. Unsettled.

ESTELA FIGUEROA, 'The Fly'.

This story
is a little peculiar.
But that's how it is.
It's our story.
And when I've told it to you
it will be a part of you
forever.

GERMANO ZULLO and ALBERTINE,
My Little One.

1

My sister likes to send me packages. It's ridiculous, because we live far apart and most of the things she sends get ruined on the way. 'Far' is too short a word once it is translated into geography: five thousand three hundred kilometres is the distance separating me from my family. My family is her. And my mother, but I don't have any contact with my mother. I don't think my sister does, either. She hasn't mentioned her in years, though I assume she still takes care of all her affairs. Sometimes I wonder about what happened to the house we lived in as children, but I don't ask, because the answer could come with information I'd rather not have.

The house was in a fishing village some ways from the city, on a sandy promontory that bit into the sea like a fang. The plot of land was large and the house was small, perched on an embankment that looked out over a savage sea that spat skates and smashed moray eels against the sea wall. The most abiding memory I have of that house is from one night when my mother went out and took a long time coming back. I must have been around five years old, my sister ten. Eusebio, the caretaker, brought her back at dawn. He said he'd found her walking along the highway. My mother's excuse was that she had gone out for some air and time had got away from her. For as long as I can remember, my mother has needed air: I recall her opening doors and windows of the house, fanning herself with brisk, wild movements. I always pictured her body as containing a flock of birds flapping to get out, scratching at her from inside. And that's why she wept. And if you tried to console her – an action that, specifically, was just a slow approach with a fearful gaze – she would skitter off like a lizard and lock herself in the bathroom.

I talk to my sister once every fortnight, plus birthdays. Also, she has the courtesy to call whenever the Caribbean is lashed by a hurricane – which I'm rarely aware of until she calls – to let me know they didn't feel a breeze. We have short, well-intentioned conversations. She always ends by announcing she's getting a package ready for me, and she lists its contents and shows me the drawings her three children have made for me, in which I'm always depicted with enormous lips, flowered dresses, golden capes, crowns, and some eye-catching cowboy boots of a sort I've never owned and never would. Sometimes she tells me, 'there's a little surprise in this one,' and she tops off the parcel with a photo taken when we were little, one of the many pictures she has in the albums she keeps organized by year. It's sad that neither the drawings nor the photos reach me intact, because she puts it all into one box and the paper gets wet from the bags of pulped fruit that sweat during the trip. Some photos hold up better depending on the paper they're printed on; maybe they don't disintegrate, but the liquid blurs our faces and turns us into ghosts.

So, I usually receive packages that are perfectly wrapped, but stuffed full of rotten food.

I let my sister send me packages because refusing

them would require an explanation that she would take badly, seeing it as confirmation that distance has turned me inconsiderate. After years of absence and a shifting relationship, the safest strategy for maintaining harmony is to pretend that there are no great differences between her and me. To neutralize ourselves. This entails a significant effort on both our parts. I know how hard it is for her to act as though my life of exile seems like a normal thing and not an extravagance, *an excess of eccentricity.* And I have to casually accept certain things, like the idea that vacuum-sealing perishable products is unimportant.

'You can count on it,' she tells me now from the computer screen.

It wasn't our day to talk, but I called because I'm going to need her help to process a document required for the grant. 'Another grant?' was her immediate, pretty lukewarm response. 'But this one's in Holland,' I explained, 'first world.' 'Congratulations!' That was the predictable reply, the one I now had to circumscribe: 'I haven't got it yet.' And her: 'But you will.'

I haven't even explained what I need yet and she's already telling me yes, of course, she'll get on it ASAP. Same as other times when she has seemed eager to do me favours that she later forgets. Part of being the older sister is to transmit that enthusiastic but hazy assurance.

Every time we talk, my ideas about the fallacy of kinship are strengthened. With each phone call, my theory gains in density what it loses in clarity. I imagine my head as home to long worms that bang against the walls; worms that grow, slow and immense; worms that coil up as they grow so they can take up more and more space. I've left them there for years, hoping that time would roll over them and squash them. But time has only been a stimulant. One day I'l have worms sprouting from my head like a medusa.

'…And some of those coconut candies you like,' says my sister, closing a list I wasn't paying attention to. It's the inventory of the latest package she's sent and that should be delivered any day now. It's not even a month since the last one arrived, which strikes me as unusual, but I don't want to interrupt and ask why the rush, because it would draw out the conversation too much.

My theory is that the awareness of a blood relationship is enough to convince people that kinship is an inexhaustible resource, that it's enough for everything: to unite opposing destinies, to twist people's wills, to combat the desire to rebel, to transform lies into memories and vice versa. Or, well, to carry on an anodyne conversation. But it's not enough, not at all. Kinship is an invisible thread, and you have to picture it constantly in order to remember it's there. The last few times I saw my sister, I repeated to myself: 'we are sisters, we are sisters', like someone who can only explain a mysterious event by resorting to faith. It's different when you live with relatives – so I think whenever I see her with her progeny – and you recognize yourself every day in the faces and gestures of other people who will age along with you and who reproduce your genetic information like spores. When my sister looks at her oldest son – identical to her – I can see the satisfaction – and the relief – in her eyes: I will live in your face forever. Maybe the understanding between them isn't really so simple or automatic, but acceptance does come more quickly.

Now my sister frowns and looks away, a sign that she is thinking about how to fill the lull in the conversation. This is a moment that terrifies me. What comes next is vertigo, a free fall into banal chit-chat. And I'm not good at that. I'm bad, not because I lack the skill – I can hold long and banal conversations with other people – but bad in the sense of evil. The only antidote to banality

I know is vileness. I never learned to be compassionate with my family.

Sometimes I feel like two people live inside me, and one of those people (the good one) keeps the other in check, but sometimes she gets tired and lowers her guard and then the other (evil) one stealthily emerges, with a mad desire to wound just for the joy of it.

A few years ago, I went back to my country to renew my passport. My sister invited me to stay at her house with her family. Since she and her husband worked and the kid – back then it was just the one – went to day care, I was home alone a lot. They gave me my nephew's room, and I slept in a low little bed with Power Rangers sheets, and I had to bend over a little to look at myself in the closet mirror. Then I would go to the dining room, make some tea and sit down to write. Sometimes I took breaks to nose around. I didn't find much that was remarkable; my sister is an obvious person. Her only secret was a photograph of our father hidden in her closet. I'd seen that photo before – when I moved away from the country, she told me I could take it if I wanted. 'No, thanks, you'll take better care of it,' I told her. So why was it a secret, then? Because her son's version of the family did not include a maternal grandfather. Not a dead one, not a living one, nothing. When I asked her why she did that – edited her genealogy so capriciously – she said: 'It's complicated.'

In her closet she also had complete outfits on hangers, solid wooden ones that could support the weight – because the sets included shoes in canvas bags with handles she hung from the hanger's neck. I wondered when she chose them, if she mixed them up every once in a while or if they were invariable. Her nightstand held magazines with marked pages that she must have wanted to read or reread. In general they were articles about how to emphasize the body's virtues and hide its imperfections. It was, more or less, the kind of thing that had interested her since adolescence. That, along with the fact that she lived in the same neighbourhood where we grew up, made her house feel like a portal to the past.

When they got home, her husband – who prided himself on being a good cook – cooked, and my sister bathed their son. I wanted to help, but I didn't know how to insert myself into a settled family, with all its routines and habits. I did basic things: set the table or tell my nephew stories until one of us started to yawn – almost always me. Then I would sit with my sister and drink herbal tea and listen to her narrate her work day in exasperating detail. At that time my aunt Vicky had been dead for about a year, and my sister was still angry. But she wasn't mad at death or at life or at God – 'who took her too soon' – but rather at global warming, toxic waste, the laboratories that manufactured viruses, the radiation from antennas in the street, and everything else that could be atrophying our cells. That quotidian life we shared was a fiction, but it worked for those first days. At times it even felt nice. I got in the habit of going to the kiosk to buy Jet chocolates I would hide in places I knew my sister and her family would easily find them. They always pretended to be surprised, we all acted like we didn't know where they had come from, and my nephew would have a fit of nervous laughter, cackles of panic that got pretty out of control. Still, we didn't confess, we let him believe that an elf snuck into the house to leave treats for us. After about ten days, though, the other me appeared, the evil one, and I started to act all elegant and say ridiculous things with my nose in the air, like someone who smells things a little too much. 'Who came up with that vulgar custom of putting cheese on fish?' was what I came out with one night, rolling my eyes in disgust. My nephew understood enough that he didn't touch the plate of sea bass smothered in cheddar his father had served him. I camouflaged my outbursts with alcohol, so that someone analyzing the situation later could say: 'Poor thing, she can't handle her booze.' This was not entirely false. The more I drank, the more the evening would lose its lustre, and the more I would want to point out the dullness that enveloped us all. The night before I left, I upped the ante: 'Cream is just a disguise for lack of skill,' I said as soon as I cracked open the second beer. 'A good cook would sooner piss on his food than dump cream all over it.' And my sister rushed to throw out the chicken roulade with béchamel sauce she had made to surprise me. Then she picked up the phone to order a pizza.

Did I know my sister had spent the afternoon beating eggs, marinating bell peppers, browning garlic, and carrying out who knows how many other tasks entirely for my benefit? Of course I did. Did I know that true elegance was a blend of humility and discretion? I did not. And the fact that my sister didn't argue demonstrated that she did. Her magnanimity overwhelmed me. In the morning, outside by the taxi with my suitcase in hand, my feet submerged in a strange fog floating in the street, I apologized. But I said it quietly, not addressing anyone, and the words evaporated. I put my head out the rear window so I could see her as the car drove away: a giant little girl waiting for her parents to come pick her up. The very picture of abandonment. And me, of a fugitive. I cried the rest of the taxi ride and I also cried on the plane, until a flight attendant offered me a whisky that I used to wash down a sleeping pill.

So now I listen to her quietly, while giving mental rejoinders that only stoke my annoyance instead of tempering it. Now I listen to her and nod meekly, while

I struggle to curb the irate creature inside me who sits gnawing at her own bloody cuticles.

Any more or less sane person would consider it suspicious that I'm still bothered by such petty things as her excessive gesticulation, or that slight but consistent little cough that forces her to pause and clear her throat with a kind of growl. One time, I tried to tell all of this to my friend Marah, who sat thinking before telling me:

'Maybe growing up means learning to turn all that irritation into tenderness.'

'Hm.'

'You know how people will say "I think it's cute", and they're not being sarcastic, they're just resigned?'

'Yeah?'

'OK, well, that's a sign the person has grown up.'

So, according to Marah, I wasn't grown up. I was emotionally stunted.

'Or maybe not,' I replied. 'Maybe the irritation comes from something else, something I choose to ignore out of laziness.'

'Out of laziness?'

'Right, I'm too lazy to untangle it.'

'But why?'

'Because it takes too long, it takes forever, and usually you don't get too much out of it.'

'So,' said Marah, 'what's your solution, then?'

'Avoidance.' It sounded like I wasn't improvising, as if I had been chewing on that answer along with my nails. 'Let go of the weight and set myself free.'

That's what I do now. I pick up the computer and wander out through the glass door that leads to the terrace and that, from this angle, has a view of a building under construction several blocks down, whose hollow, reticulated structure holds little bits of sky. From far away it looks like a drawing. Work on it stopped months ago. They finished the structure, put in floor slabs, but they never got to the doors and windows. It was going to be an office building, fifty stories of concrete and glass and one of those panoramic elevators that often requires the rescue of a person with vertigo. Panicked. Covered in vomit.

My sister's frown starts to dissolve:

'Is it very hot there?' she asks.

'No, it's autumn now.'

'How nice, like in the movies.'

What movies?

'But the sun is brutal,' I say.

It's true. Through the empty windows of the grey building, *the sun burns brutal and bright.*

'Here too. Well, you know how it is, we have nonstop summer here,' she laughs half-heartedly.

Summer. Hard to call it that without any contrast. Excessive heat all year long does not count as summer.

'Well, summer's nice too, isn't it?' she says.

Summer means the rebirth of something that has died. Without death there is no life, I want to tell her. The sick leaves die off first, and it's good for them because they grow back faster, as soon as the heat returns. The healthiest ones hang on, they make it through the season and stay alive through weather that wounds them. They live more and suffer more. They are martyrs.

'I don't know if I like the summer.' I suppose she expects me to say this so she can give me a soothing answer.

'Lucky, then. Because here you wouldn't have a choice.'

The truth is my sister doesn't always fill the conversational lulls the same way. I have to admit she manages better than I do. Sometimes, when she realizes we've spent a while silent and staring off into the distance, she proceeds with a strategy I think is wise: she tells me about people I don't know, or whom I know only through her, and her stories are so repetitive it's easy for me to predict what their protagonists will do. That's how I can give accurate answers to her random questions:

'Guess what María Elvira did?' / 'Asked you to lend her money and didn't pay you back.' / 'You're psychic, you know?'

'I bet you don't know what happened to Lucho.' / 'Which Lucho?' / 'Uncle Lucho.' / 'He got drunk and someone mugged him.' / 'Exactly right!'

'Remember Patricia Piñeres's son?' / 'I think so.' / 'Well…' / 'He's gay.' / 'Yep!'

'Melissa, my sister-in-law, quit her job.' / 'Why? Is she pregnant again?' / 'Holy Mary! How do you do that?'

But that doesn't happen today. She doesn't tell me anything about anyone. When she notices my silence she goes quiet and sighs. I guess she, too, gets fed up with the weight of incomprehension. I guess that on top of seeming like a sister who is *detached, dejected, and discourteous*, I also come off as an arrogant person. Kinship isn't enough for her, either, of course it isn't. In cases like ours, getting along isn't a question of magic or chemistry or affinity, but of *tenacity, toughness, and torturous toiling*.

Sometimes avoidance consists of imagining a black hole in my thoughts, into which I toss tricky lists of words that are similar in form and meaning. In any case, avoidance is always a dumb game that helps me shift focus.

'Well, your package should be there soon,' she says, as a preamble to ending the call.

That's when I notice her clothes: more formal than on other days, everything in shades of beige like she's dressed for a baptism. She has straightened her hair and it's lighter than last time, with no roots showing. It's a miracle her hair still grows at all after she used straightener for so many years, and so constantly that my aunt Vicky had to make aloe compresses to soothe the irritation on her scalp. My sister is white like meringue, but her hair is fiercely kinky; according to my grandmother, that is the only true sign of blackness. Much of her adolescence was dedicated to eradicating that trait, even if she had to maim her scalp to do it.

'Are you going somewhere?' I ask her.

There is no ambient noise from her end, which makes me think her kids and husband aren't there, and neither is that annoying dog that sheds everywhere. Today is Saturday, and usually they would all be there, buzzing around in the corners like cicadas.

'We're going on the cruise.'

'Where?'

'I told you, we're taking a cruise.'

And how they're just so happy because there are tons of activities for the kids, she says. And there's a movie theatre with a monster screen; a wave pool and regular pools; chefs from all around the world; yoga classes; an awesome spa; brand name stores; two galas…'

'What about the dog?'

'The neighbours are watching him, the kids are taking him round as we speak.'

'You're going now?'

'The ship leaves in two hours, but we still have to get to the port.'

'Right.'

'OK, take care.' She leans towards the screen and makes a loud kissing sound.

'Happy travels,' I reply, but her face has disappeared. I see only my own face reflected on the screen, wearing that expression of indignation I get when I feel like I've missed something.

Where was the cruise ship headed? When did she plan this? Is it a spontaneous trip? Did she win it?

I remember my document, the urgent errand, the reason for my call.

Marah would have said that, just maybe, the urgency wasn't real.

How do you mean?

Did I *really* want to go to Holland?

Yes, I wanted to.

What for?

To write.

But what did I do here?

Same thing, but with suffering.

And what about that guy I'd been dating for, how long now? Two, three months? Didn't he make me question it a little?

No.

Not even a little?

No.

No?

2

I live in a seventh-floor apartment with a view interrupted by treetops and some modern skyscrapers newly built along the block. Almost right across from me, or more like diagonally, there's a building of high-ceilinged lofts with a steel and glass façade. The lofts are expensive, pretentious, and tiny. From my window I can see everything that happens inside the only unit that faces towards me; the inhabitants are a couple and their baby. They're not home today. They left last night with a couple of cloth bags and the collapsible pushchair, and, as usual, they left the light on to throw off who knows who. 'Maybe they do it so they won't trip when they get back,' Axel said as we watched them leave from my terrace. We were sitting in a couple of plastic chairs set far back from the railing, because he's afraid of heights. Last night was the third time Axel came to my place. Usually we go to his, which is better equipped and doesn't have a balcony.

I don't like it when the neighbours leave. Then I have to look at other windows where the view is more diffuse. I don't think they like leaving, either; they always look grumpy when they come back. They shift the baby from arm to arm and he cries, because he can sense their discomfort. They, in turn, are bewildered by his crying: they rock him very fast, they turn pale and look like they're about to lose it, until the baby quietens down and they can breathe again. I don't know how they can recover their equilibrium when it slips away so easily, right before their eyes like an onslaught of midges.

Now I'm resting my elbows on the balcony railing. I'm not afraid of heights; on the contrary, taking in the view from up high soothes me. Down below, the doorman is sweeping the building's entrance. He is wearing brown overalls that, seen from above, make him look like one of those round bugs that smell bad. Stinkbugs, they're called. He looks up, squints into the bright sky, and catches me looking at him. I wave, and he leans against the broom to wave back. There's a slow but constant shower of yellow leaves falling. I wait for him to turn around and go on with his work. Máximo — that's the doorman's name — can spend the whole day sweeping. And in that exercise a ball of bitterness gradually builds up in the pit of his stomach. The kind of bitterness that over time will lead a person to grab the nearest stick and beat the shit out of a dog or an old man.

The sun shines through the foliage and I leave the terrace.

The forecast is for rain all weekend, though there's not a whiff of it now. I don't plan to go out. I'm going to make do with a can of tuna and an apple, and I'm going to spend all afternoon sitting here writing the grant proposal. I have ten days to send it.

I pace lazily around the apartment: kitchen, living room, bedroom, bathroom, bedroom, living room, kitchen. If my footsteps left marks on the floor, they would make a narrow U-shape. My apartment is tiny, too, but in a more proletarian way than the ones across from me. I try hard to keep it bare of any decoration because I'm afraid that if I don't watch myself, I'll display a provincial taste that I reject but that, deep down, I know I possess and could rear up at the slightest provocation. So I try to keep it clean and curated, favouring functional elements that for the most part live in the kitchen. I disguise my ignorance with minimalism.

The only thing in this space that elides that austere vocation is a Chesterfield sofa that takes up the whole room designated as living-dining. The Chesterfield is my visitors' couch, my chaise longue for naps, my desk and my dining table. I bought it at a garage sale held at a rich old lady's house after she died. The sale was announced on a page I had subscribed to that occasionally sent me notifications for auctions that I didn't attend. I always found that the things I liked were too expensive, and the things I could afford were painful because they only reminded me of my precariousness. I went to this one because the dead old lady had the same name as me, and that coincidence was enough to convince me to go – though it wasn't so strange: my name, at least in this city, is old-fashioned. When I arrived, the sofa had already been sold. That's what the woman in charge told me with a determined toss of her crown of red ringlets, and then she tried to sell me a set of tarnished silverware as a consolation prize. Then the dead woman's son appeared; he had some kind of mental condition, and so no one paid him much mind when he hawked the bric-a-brac displayed on a garden table, the sector he'd been relegated to by that cruel redheaded woman. But it was clear the man couldn't stand the disappointment that came over my face; he led me outside, insisting on showing me some mouldy parasols, and he took a little card from his pocket with the sofa's brand and model, plus the words 'purchased by' and a name that had been crossed out. I had to replace it with my information and then drop it in the sales urn. 'It's yours,' he said in his languid modulation, handing me the card with a gesture that was like a bow. And that was how we perpetrated a fraud that cost me dearly: between the price of the sofa and the moving truck rental, I spent my budget for two months.

The sofa is so out of place in my living room that it has a certain flair. Its purpose is to isolate me in a bubble of false sophistication, incomprehensible to most of the people who come into my house. Just last night, Axel asked if I wasn't a countess fallen on hard times, 'or something like that'. He laughed. I sat watching his face fall as he grew more discomfited by my silence. 'Joke,' he clarified. I was thinking about the hollowness of that expression: 'or something like that'. Something like what? In the end I gave him one of those generic replies that could be applied to a range of questions: no one is interested enough in looking, I told him, and that's why some people got a false idea of my tastes and my home (really, I said *fatuous and false*, and my memory is editing out the redundancy), which only reinforced my lack of desire to explain myself to others. When I finished talking I felt stupid and I must have looked stupid, because he didn't stay to sleep over. In the meantime, we talked about other things that I can't remember now. We entered into a dance of ambiguity that ruined everything.

It's noon; my sister must be aboard her cruise ship by now. I can just see her gazing excitedly at the array of interactive screens showing maps of the ship marked with little flags: '…over twenty stations of international food.'

I wonder: When my sister isn't there, who takes care of my mother?

I can't find the tuna in the kitchen. The pantry holds salted peanuts and tortilla chips. I open the fridge: water, cookies, a jar of olives in brine. I take the olives and chips and set them on the floor beside the sofa, next to the laptop, and go to the bathroom. As I'm standing up from the toilet I'm surprised at the sight of my face in the mirror over the sink. I see something new there. A pent-up expression waiting to be set free. Fear, I think. Fear of what? Something tells me I've looked like this for longer than just a morning. Months? Years? I rub my face. I brush my hair, shoo away that idea, turn my back on the mirror and return to the living room. I sit on the sofa and look out the window: a listless sky, still free of rainclouds. I press my thumb into the middle of my palm until I feel a pinch and let go.

A bang on the glass wakes me up, but there's nothing outside. It's raining – the wind must have shaken the sliding door that leads to the terrace. I get up from the sofa and switch on the floor lamp, but it doesn't work. I guess the electricity went out in the storm. I hear another blow, and when I look outside I see a man in a hood standing there. I take two quick steps backwards and bump into the lamp, which falls to the floor, smashing the bulb. The man knocks with both hands, then takes off the hood of his raincoat:

'It's Máximo,' he says.

It's Máximo, I tell myself, but I'm still paralyzed. There are nights when everything seems like a threat.

'Are you OK?' he asks, his voice filtered through the rain and the glass.

I nod, but it's dark and he can't see me. I pick up the fallen lamp, use my foot to sweep the shards of glass into a little pile in a corner. Then I open the sliding door.

'What's wrong?'

Máximo is soaked. He'd had to come up to the terrace to get to the fuse box because a fuse blew, he says.

'OK,' I say.

He'd used the fire escape, he hadn't meant to scare me. He goes on talking as he heads for the fuse box. Before turning to the constellation of orange buttons, he asks me again:

'Are you OK?'

'Yes, yes.' And I offer him a cup of coffee that he accepts.

The electricity comes back on, and I go to the kitchen to make the coffee. When I come back, Máximo is leaning in the threshold of the sliding door. He doesn't want to come in because he'll track water and mess up the floor, he explains. He's going to take the fire escape back down, same way he came up. I nod.

'Did you get the crate?' he asks after taking a big sip of coffee.

'What crate?'

'You didn't get it?'

'No.'

'It's really big.' He finishes the coffee and hands me the mug without a thanks or anything. The disdainful gesture, plus the mention of the size of the crate (which, I assume, is the package from my sister), reminds me of the day I moved into this apartment: how hard it was to wrangle in the Chesterfield where I'm sitting now, watching him rub his hands together for warmth.

The operation consisted, firstly, of wrapping the sofa in a very thick cling film that compressed it significantly, though still not enough to fit in the elevator or up the stairs. So I had to hire a service to have men with harnesses attach it to ropes and hoist it up outside, while they flew like Tinkerbells escorting the sofa to the terrace. It was an acrobatics show that I filmed from start to finish. Máximo disapproved of the whole thing. He thought it was risky, capricious, and very silly: 'It's not even a nice sofa,' he told me in one of the many arguments we had about it. To soften him up, I bought a box of chocolates and a card that said 'Thank you' in shiny capital letters. He took it with the same expression he wears when he takes complaints from the condo association, and he didn't miss the chance to tell me that things aren't done like that here. By 'here' he meant his country, which isn't mine; by 'like that' he meant any way that did not recognize him as a sovereign authority.

'It was delivered it in the afternoon, I let the guys in. Four of them brought it up, because it's made of wood, really heavy.' He takes a breath, as if the mere telling had exhausted him. 'They used those dollies with handles, but still.'

'Right.' I take another sip from my empty cup.

Máximo nods and looks at the apartment's front door. He juts his chin towards it:

'It must be out there in the hallway.'

3

Sunday morning is sunny, but I'm still inside.

From my bed I can see a slice of imperfect sky: the blue clipped by skinny clouds that break apart like steam in the shower. Finally they take the shape of rags drying in the breeze and I lose interest, but I don't get up until the phone rings.

'Are they back yet?' It's Axel. He's the only one who calls the landline: an old cordless phone that was already in the apartment when I rented it.

'Who?' My mind flashes on Catrina, the building's cat, who disappeared a few weeks ago. But Axel used the plural. Plus, I'm not sure I've told him about Catrina.

'The couple across from you,' he says.

I dreamed about Catrina.

'Oh, hang on, let me see.' I go out to the terrace and look: no change. 'They're not back.'

'OK. So, what're you doing?'

'Gathering momentum. I need to work later.'

'On what?'

Nor have I told him about applying for a grant that, if I can manage to send the proposal in time, I'm very likely to get. Why? Because I'm cheap and appealing:

single, young, Latina. And especially because I know the director, who personally invited me to apply: '*It's perfect for you*,' she said. If I get the grant, I'll move to Holland for a year that, as I see it, could stretch to three, or seven, or ten. Axel knows none of this.

'Something new,' I tell him. 'I'm still not sure what it is.'

I have breakfast on the terrace. First I have to dry the plastic table and open the umbrella, which is soaked and leaves me drenched. I go inside to change, grab a blanket in case it turns chilly, and get the laptop. When I come back outside Catrina is there, and I pounce on her. Maybe it wasn't a dream; maybe she was meowing outside my window all night long. People in the building have given her up for dead and they all blame me, though no one has accused me to my face. Well, except for León, the kid from the first floor who I take care of sometimes because his mom, a nurse, often has to stay late at the emergency room, and his babysitter goes to a night-time high school. 'My mom says you ate the cat,' León told me one morning a few days ago. We were both in the building's lobby (him waiting for the school bus, me for a Cabify). I smiled, taking pity on the kid and saving my retort for his mother. 'No one stays at the ER so late unless they're sleeping with the doctor on duty.' That's what León's babysitter had told me one of those nights when she had to hand him off to me, ready for bed in moose-printed pyjamas though with no intention of going to sleep.

Catrina made the rounds of all the apartments, but she had a clear preference for my terrace. When it was brought up at the building meeting whether the cat should be adopted by someone or should wander at will (and be considered the property's pet), all eyes turned to me, putting the weight of the decision on my shoulders. It was logical to think that one person could perfectly well take care of a cat, said Carla, the woman who presided over the meetings. After all, cats were independent animals that didn't need anything beyond water and food and an old rag to sleep on. Same as a hobo, I thought, and yet no one would ask you to take care of one.

'Catrina, where were you?'

I pick her up and hug her. The cat lets me pet her but looks at me gravely, as if she bears news but can't bring herself to tell me.

'What's wrong, Catrina? Tell me, please.'

She loses interest and scrambles off to the corner where her bedding is, but finds it wet and dirty. Though she's not allowed in the apartment, she goes in and jumps onto the Chesterfield with utter impunity. I go to the kitchen for food and water and put the bowls on the terrace thinking she'll follow me, but she stays on the sofa watching my movements with wide eyes. Before sitting at the table to work I give her one more glance, and I feel something new, a sort of relief or unexpected warmth. Then I scan the terrace: I'm looking for leaves to sweep, more water to wipe up. Any excuse to put off writing. The terrace looks clean and feels welcoming, just like the first time I saw it and thought how extravagant – in the best possible way – I found this space: the terrace takes up half the area of my apartment. Who can allow themselves that? One half, the inside one, is divided into three rooms that are like office cubicles: the bedroom with its bathroom; the living-dining room; and the kitchen with a small laundry room that I use for storage. The other half is just this: emptiness. When I moved in I was tempted to buy plants, but I stopped myself in time. The place would have been taken over by dried-out vegetation, because I wouldn't have bothered to pull the withered stems from their pots. I adore other people's gardens, the orchids and orange blossoms and lush ferns; I adore the shining green of new leaves. There are days when I look out at the balcony of the couple with the baby and am overcome with wonder at their flowers, so fresh and colourful and unruly. Sometimes I wait for darkness just to get a glimpse of the imprecise shapes of those plants against the wall. They look relaxed, mischievous, freed from their decorative obligation. But I'm less attracted to the idea of tending a garden of my own, because I feel that in my hands, any new shoot would lose its vitality just as fast as I'd lose interest.

I have three paragraphs written and I already know they won't work. When I start out I'm dull, or maybe unfocused. Not enough that I don't realize it, but enough that I'm unable to fix it. Catrina comes out to the terrace and lolls belly up in a beam of sunlight. She looks fatter and I wonder where she's been, what she has eaten, whether some friendly hand has stroked her fur all these nights.

The first time Catrina appeared on the terrace, she brought me a sock stolen from some neighbour's clothesline as an offering. I used that same sock to make her a ball that's still around here somewhere, hairy and covered in grime. Later she brought handkerchiefs, t-shirts, a child's sandal, a buttered roll.

I get up from the table and nudge her food bowl closer, but she still ignores it.

I lean against the balcony again. The skeleton of the building under construction strikes me as a beautiful view. I hope they never finish it. Catrina comes over to rub against my legs and purr. I look at her and think that we are in one of those rare coincidences of satisfaction: Catrina is happy and I am calm, which is almost the same thing. We are enough for each other. Neither of us seems to want to be anywhere else. But then the front door buzzer startles her and she bolts inside. From the balcony I can see that it's Máximo and I don't feel like answering, so I step back from the railing before he sees me. I return to the computer, reread two paragraphs. The door buzzes again and I ignore it. I try to keep reading but the noise distracted me, cooled me off, distanced me. When that happens it's hard to get going again, to remember that what I'm doing matters to me and has a reason to exist. Because the truth is it *does* matter to me, but it has no reason to exist. Still, if I make an effort and really focus, I can invent a convincing one.

Damned Máximo.

I go to the kitchen to make mate.

I fill the electric kettle with water, turn it on, get the yerba and sugar, waste time. I take in air, inflate myself with determination.

'I have to write,' I tell Catrina, who is following me.

The application consists of two parts, of which the first, I presume, is the most important. It involves an explanation of my project, what I'm proposing to write during the period of my residency. But I'm still not sure about that, so I start with the second part, which, in theory, is easier: Write a piece on your feelings about writing. This could be terrible. Or brilliant. Depends on who's answering. And although writing is something I have done every day for years now, I again get the feeling that this thing I call 'my job' is nothing but another avoidance strategy. Compared to all other professions, writing is like the effort a tick makes to feed and survive among predators. I climb up onto a branch, wait a long time until the herd passes, calculate the least risky distance to drop onto a fluffy mass and drink a minuscule ration of blood, which will allow me to maintain this limited but sufficient life.

My job is small. And a little contemptible, too.

Sometimes the awareness of that smallness can be mistaken for resentment. When anyone more or less close to me inquires as to the real prospects for my writing, my explanation is so abstract that it can be read as a complaint or a resigned retort. One night, León was sprawled on the Chesterfield while I squeezed against the armrest to finish writing a piece that had hijacked my head. He was almost asleep when he asked me, 'What do you do?' And although I had already explained it in multiple ways that night and others, I repeated, 'I'm a writer.' And with the most sincere befuddlement, he asked: 'You get paid for that?'

I would have liked to tell León how that was not the important thing. That my work mattered to me because I believed there was more truth coursing through those vestigial professions than through the central and important ones. There were jobs that made you think you had the power to create change on a grand scale. An engineer must feel a little like that: magnanimous. In smaller trades, on the other hand, there was an effort at synthesis that translated into a kind of essence. This essence was not magnanimous, but forcibly concentrated. You either saw it or you ignored it, which you couldn't do with a bridge. I didn't need to convince myself that the screw I oiled every day was important in the great machinery that powered the universe. I knew full well that if I didn't oil that screw, no one would miss it. Yes, of course I harboured some resentment, just like most of humanity. Every one of my sentences hid furious warriors itching to shoot off a round of arrows. But I held them in check, kept their fury on the sidelines.

'Sometimes,' I told León. He was already asleep.

First I hear the door buzzer, and then come the knocks on the door. One after another: hard, loud.

I get up from the table on the terrace and go uneasily inside.

'Who is it?' I ask. I look through the peephole but can't see anything, because something is covering it.

'It's Máximo.'

I open the door and something comes at me, a gigantic cube that I have to stop with my body.

'All the neighbours are complaining because this is blocking the way, people can't get through,' says Máximo.

'What?'

My only neighbours are the married couple next door. That 'all' is a provocation.

'It was delivered almost two days ago, and it's still sitting out here.'

The weight of the box is too much for me.

'Can you help me, Máximo, please? It's really heavy.'

Máximo snorts. He slides in on one side between the box and the wall and grabs it long-ways with his arms outstretched. He says 'excuse me' but still pushes me with his body, which is bulky like a bulldozer, and he half-drags, half-lifts the box inside and drops it onto the sofa, sideways.

'What is this?' I ask.

Máximo snorts again. He takes a handkerchief out of his trouser pocket and wipes his sweaty face. He mutters on his way out and slams the door behind him.

Catrina jumps on top of the box, sniffs it, and licks it.

'Catrina,' I yell. 'Shoo!'

But the cat doesn't run, just gives me a look that's different from the one a while ago on the terrace. I sit on the floor, facing her.

'What's up, Catrina?'

In her enormous eyes I find a dark and shifting pool

where I can see myself reflected. I close my eyes and open them again and I think I see, in the same reflection, someone else's face. I close and open them again, just to make sure the pool in the cat's eyes never stays still. That's why I'm different every time I peer into them.

I call Axel, because Máximo is ignoring me.

'I don't have any of the things you're asking for,' he tells me.

'Not even a hammer?'

'I might have a hammer.'

I'll need tools to open the crate. Ideally a Phillips-head screwdriver so I can remove the screws and disassemble the box: I looked it up online. First, I tried to pry it open with the sharpest knife in my kitchen, and when I stuck it under the board that serves as a lid and levered it upward, the tip of the knife broke off.

'Can you come over?'

'It'll have to be later, sorry. I'm at my parents' house.'

It's Sunday. Normal people are with their families, eating and getting depressed.

I met Axel's parents once, when we ran into them at the grocery store near his house – they live in the same neighbourhood. I guess he feels responsible for them because his only sister moved to Australia or New Zealand (I can never remember which). Axel's parents are both tall, him a little taller than her. They look like generic actors – good looking, up to a point. Nothing in their appearance that day seemed all that noteworthy, except for their composure, their flat elegance of plain sweaters, khaki (his) and lilac (hers). The encounter was uncomfortable because the mother never stopped smiling. Easy laughter makes me nervous; it's confusing and distorts the laughing person. The father seemed more normal, or at least more restrained in his mannerisms. Axel was so nervous he practically didn't talk. He kept running his hand through his hair and looking at the shelves, searching for some non-existent product. His parents' cart was overflowing with food: there were, in particular, a lot of condiments that struck me as daring for their age. The mother was holding a set of plastic cups that said 'Cheers!' So there's a possible classification, I thought: Axel's mother belongs to the group of people who buy objects that speak. Bowls with the word 'Salad', smaller bowls with the word 'Snacks'. When we were about to part ways, the mother went to give Axel a kiss and he ducked it accidentally because he didn't see it coming. I felt bad for her, and embarrassed; she just hugged her cups and walked away. For the first time, I thought about Axel as a child. When I meet the parents of someone close to me, I can't help but imagine the boy or girl they once were, bring them onstage to pose beside their older incarnation. Something about that picture oppresses me. Parents are the peephole you look through to spy on childhood.

I look back at the crate: it takes up the whole sofa, which is to say the whole living room. It nullified the only useful room in the apartment. The word 'Fragile' is printed in red on all its sides.

At six I call Axel again, but he doesn't answer.

I imagine him watching TV with his parents, ensconced in a too-cushy sofa, suffocated by the heat in a house that, as he's told me, they can't manage to keep at a moderate temperature. It's always too hot or too cold, so they have to be forever mindful of the thermostat, and can never really relax. It's easier to ignore the heat, Axel thinks, because it sneaks up on you: it gives you gentle little taps that daze you but don't knock you out. Not as fast. The cold is rougher. The cold pierces your flesh until it hits bone.

I call him again. No answer.

I prefer the cold for exactly the same reasons Axel gives. I'll take its roughness and expediency over the sneakiness of heat. The cold doesn't fool you, doesn't play around, doesn't overpower you slowly. I grew up in the heat, gradually suffocating. Often, when I ask my sister 'how are you?' she answers 'waterlogged.' It seems like the perfect image to describe the state of bodies in that climate.

After looking at the crate for a while and trying to discern a secret mechanism to open it, I give up. I want to go back to the terrace, and on the way I grab a sweatshirt, a black one that says 'Rabid Fox' on the chest. It got left behind on the hook in the bathroom months ago. I was going to give it away to someone in the street, but one day it snuck into the bag I brought to the laundromat, and it came back folded and smelling of Woolite. It's too big for me, but I really like it. It belonged to a guy I was going out with before Axel: *one* of the guys I was going out with before Axel. They were unaware of their proximity, and I, who had never gone out with two guys at once, felt transgressive, voracious, guilty, and adrenaline-charged. What a deal, I thought: I give so little and get so much. But then I met Axel, and it was easy to leave them both because neither seemed all that upset. Although my first reaction to the ease of undoing a relationship was to take silent offence, I thought about it later and decided that those were probably the most civilized relationships I'd ever had. I appreciated the affectionate indifference with which A and B said good-bye to me: A with a long hug; B with a kiss and the sweatshirt I'm now wearing. The detail of the sweatshirt is important: it's a way to flaunt a secret I'm keeping to myself. I always think the memory of that double relationship is going to age well. But one day I'll likely give in to the temptation of blowing it out of proportion, and a severe voice in my head will have to admonish me: they weren't any big thing, it's just that they didn't hurt you. There's no virtue in not hurting you, it's almost the opposite. To hurt someone, you need cruelty – that is, genuine interest. It's easy not to hurt; usually all you have to do is abstain.

Taking care of someone is a virtue – letting go of something valuable and not expecting it to return.

And loving, they say, is more or less the same thing.

Does Axel love me?

They also say love matures into gratitude. So I will be grateful to anyone who makes me love, even if they haven't loved me. If that's true, whether Axel loves me or not, I tell myself – lie to myself? forewarn myself? console myself? – is completely irrelevant.

I go out on the terrace; I want to focus on the application.

I could not reproduce the reasoning of love in written words – couldn't type the words 'love', 'loved', 'loves' – without my fingers getting coated in treacle. If I wanted to talk about love, I would replace that word with another. Which one? Bewilderment, that's what occurs to me now. I feel dizzy. Sometimes that happens to me with words. Like being a carpenter who's allergic to sawdust. There are words I have forbidden myself, more and more of them all the time, and I have trouble finding new ones to replace them. I know very few words. And I don't go around carrying a magnifying glass and dragging dictionaries with me. It's even worse than that: I go around hopeful, convinced that the words I'm looking for are just going to come and hit me over the head.

I sigh. It smells like jasmine outside. Must be the last flowers. Or the first.

There's not much left of the afternoon. Short days, long nights, everything starts over again. Nature doesn't advance, it repeats, it dances in circles, it buffers.

I yawn in hunger.

A round and premature moon emerges.

4

At eight-thirty I get up from the table to stretch my legs and look out from the balcony. Two women in track suits – florescent pink and florescent orange – go by at an athletic pace on the street below. They leave a zigzagging wake behind them that makes them look like fireflies. Lightening bugs, *bichitos de luz*, as they're called around here. Then I see a boy standing on the sidewalk, looking down at the lit screen of his phone while his dog sniffs at his feet. This isn't a very busy street, but there's always something happening. I look inside, towards the living room: it's dark. Because, I remember now, the floor lamp broke. Where is Catrina? Did she run off again? The box is still on the sofa. Tomorrow I'll have to find some way to open it or get rid of it. Maybe I'll call the church and donate it, still sealed. There is nothing I need that could be inside that box.

My mouth feels dry from all the chips and olives.

I made some progress in my application. Not much.

I head inside for something to drink. I cross the threshold and fumble on the wall for the switch for the overhead light, which I never use since it's too harsh.

Then I see her.

I turn off the light. It's a reflex.

Shadows from outside tremble on the walls.

I turn on the light again. There she is: sitting in the middle of the sofa, her hair smoothed back in a tight bun that pulls at her temples and leaves her dark face clear – eyelashes stiff with mascara, bright blush on her cheeks, earth-coloured lips. I see her framed against a clean background as though painted on canvas. She's wearing a sleeveless dress, and she's hugging herself and rubbing her arms.

'I'm cold,' she says.

The box has been taken apart into its six panels, piled one atop the other.

'I'm cold,' she repeats.

So I run to my room and bring her a shawl that she puts over her shoulders, and then she turns to me with that troubled look I thought I'd got rid of years ago.

'I don't understand,' I say finally, faced with her unchanging expression.

'Don't you worry,' she shakes her head with a mixture of sadness and indignation. 'If you'll just call me a cab, I can head back right away.'

Even in my confusion, I see the humour in her words.

My mother always was, above all else, a dependent woman. She needed help for everything, and even with help, practical life demanded an outsized effort from her.

'I don't want to bother you.' She is still rubbing her arms over the wrap.

I go out to the terrace to get the laptop. Catrina is lying on the warm keyboard. I sit down at the table feeling dizzy. I want water. I pet the cat and realize my fingers are trembling. I look out at the hollow building. I imagine codes starting to appear inside those little squares, codes I have to decipher. I pick up the cat and move her to the floor. She walks off towards the wall separating my terrace from that of the neighbours, the married couple. She jumps to the other side and disappears again. Before going back inside, I convince myself that the apartment is empty. It's all just a glitch, I think, one of those tiny fissures in reality that lets something seep in that later on, because we don't have the vocabulary for it, we call 'delirium'.

I open the sliding door, and there's no one inside. The box isn't there either. I take a deep breath, overcome by such an intense feeling of relief that it seems funny, though I don't laugh. I feel high. I can't trust my own senses. I hear water running in the kitchen sink. Is she washing the dishes? What dishes? Nothing is dirty. My mother was bad at washing dishes: her countertops always had a thick patina, geological layers of grease.

I peer through the kitchen door: on my counter, containers I don't recognize are dripping dry. The concentrated air in the small room feels thick and smells like soup, like beef stew, like coriander and garlic. There's nothing cooking on the stove, and none of those products are in the refrigerator. Her presence makes me call up those smells. Without daring to enter the room I ask:

'Are you hungry?'

She shakes her head.

'Are you tired?'

'A little.'

'I'll make up my bed for you.'

'Don't put yourself out.'

'I'll sleep on the sofa.'

'No, that's OK.'

'In any case, I have to work.'

'I can sleep in any old corner.'

'It's decided.'

'I'm not even tired.'

I go to the bedroom, strip the old sheets off the bed and put new ones on. Then I remove any objects that could get in her way: books on the bedside table, hair ties, a notebook, a pencil case, condoms, arnica cream for tired feet, sandals. I put it all into a tote bag, tie the handles together, and stash it on the upper shelf in the closet. I move quickly but surely, as though covering up the scene of a crime. Then I go into the bathroom for a clean towel that I hang on the hook. On one side of the shower I place shampoo, soap, a shower cap.

My mother is busy making arepas for dinner. She puts cheese and butter on them and tops them with chopped mint leaves. We drink beers, two each, and neither of us speaks, neither of us asks any questions. I guess I can tolerate this for a while. After dinner she agrees to lie down in my bed. She's not hard to convince: her pride is a fragile shell. While she settles into the bedroom, I go to the shelf in the living room to get a book for her. I have a hard time choosing because I can't remember what she likes. I pick up *A Lost Lady*, but I'm afraid the title alone will predispose her against it. I leave it on the shelf. Too bad, because it's a beautiful book. When I come back she is kneeling beside the bed, murmuring a prayer. I let her finish before I speak:

'Do you need anything?'

'Cats spread disease, sweetheart,' she whispers.

'Say what?'

'I saw you have a cat.'

Her voice shakes; she is nervous. I can almost hear the flock of birds in her chest. Her forehead shines with sweat. Back when I lived with her, whenever we were alone in a room together, my mother had a hard time talking to me. She would give me a strange look without saying a word. I didn't feel responsible for generating any kind of conversation: I was the daughter, I was a kid. So there we'd sit, stretching out the silence until I got bored or fell asleep, and she took her chance to leave.

'Her name is Catrina,' I reply, 'and she's not mine, she belongs to the building.'

I leave the room, walk through the kitchen and open the window to air the place out. Then I go into the laundry room to do the same, and I find the disassembled box: its parts are propped clumsily against the walls. I snort. Madness, it's a fit of madness.

I leave the apartment and the building, walk six blocks to the neighbourhood park. Leafy and wild and full of *crotos* – that's what they call hobos around here – especially at night. I sit on a bench and wonder who I could tell all this to. Marah? We haven't seen each other in a while. I can't call and throw something like this at her. Our last meeting was rough. We'd planned to get together at a bar downtown near her work, but I was late and we fought. We got pretty carried away, I don't even remember why. Probably because of the shitty attitude she takes on every time I start dating someone. Marah is possessive and jealous. 'Just admit the fact you're a lesbo,' I told her. She thought that was a comment that could only come from a deformed brain corroded by categories: 'you're a narrow-minded, binary basic bitch.' It got too late to catch the subway and we shared a taxi that dropped us off in this very park, but on the other side. We had to cross it at a run, afraid we'd be assaulted. We went so fast that I couldn't see anything but flashes of the landscape floating in the darkness. Marah shouted and I laughed – the alcohol had mutated into a crazy, childish excitement. Later she confessed that she'd put a tab of acid in the water we drank in the taxi. I had drunk almost all of it. It hit me hard. Since that night, every once in a while my nose bleeds.

An old man is walking towards me. He's dirty and ragged. I stand up to walk away and the old man shouts: 'A cigarette! Gimme a cigarette!' I run out of the park and back to my building. The moon is losing its edges, but in the centre it's still white and shining. My neighbours, the married couple, are in the building lobby. We get in the elevator together and greet each other with a nod of the head. That old-fashioned, polite gesture only confirms our absolute lack of affinity. They seem pretentious and self-absorbed to me. I don't even want to think about how I seem to them.

'Did you see the cat?' I ask them.

'No,' the woman says. 'Did she come back?'

'Yeah, she was on my terrace, but then she went over to yours.'

They exchange a look, as though asking each other if they'd seen the animal.

'We didn't see her,' the woman says with a worried expression.

'Maybe she kept going,' I reply. 'She'll be back.'

We exit the elevator and say good night. I put the key into my front door.

'Whatever you were cooking earlier smelled really good,' I hear the man say.

I look at them and nod, then go inside. Again, I pray that no one is there, that the universe has self-corrected during my walk. My mother is in bed, just as I left her but with my white blanket pulled up to her chin.

Where is her luggage?

Her breath has poisoned the room with that familiar smell of wilted flowers. My mother exhales passionflower, a homeopathic tincture for the nerves. She used to guzzle it down, her only prescription a desire to lose consciousness. 'Booze would be worse,' my sister used to say, but we both figured our mother didn't have the guts to drink for real.

How long does she plan to stay?

Her sleeping face doesn't betray any torment. I think how that placid mantle is only seen in sleep, because sleep does not belong to us. There is something else that controls it. Something external and foreign. A force that is *invisible, inaccessible, incomprehensible, immense.* There's that tic again. The succession of almost identical words that emerge from my mouth like gobs of spit.

Did she bring any money?

I close the door, lie down on the sofa, and look outside, and I see Catrina on the terrace. She takes a few quick strides until she's very close to the sliding door. She is carrying something in her mouth, but I can't make out what it is until she drops it on the ground and licks her mouth clean: it's a medium-sized rat, its belly bleeding where she bit into it.

5

The sound of the shower wakes me up. It's Monday, and on Mondays I have to go to an advertising agency I do some freelance jobs for. They almost always have me write about food: anything from nutritional information to product history, which tends to be the distillation of a pompous myth cooked up by the client. I can't work regular daily hours at the agency, because I have a sketchy contract with no benefits, and they're afraid that someday, if I ever built up enough desire or desperation, I'd be able to stick them with a lawsuit. So I go to meetings, they assign me one-off projects, and then they send me away with pats on the back, words of encouragement, a compliment that almost always verges on the inappropriate, and a bag with free samples of things I don't need. That's why the bathroom drawer is full of acne products, hair colour diluter, organic makeup, and Xanax. I like to go in because it gets me out of my pyjamas and my house, it forces me to shower and go to a restaurant to eat lunch off a plate instead of straight from Tupperware on the terrace.

I get up from the sofa and open the blinds. It's a cloudy day; it's going to be cold.

The rat is still there, its blood dry and its eyes wide open, as though in fear. I want to get rid of it before my mom sees it, so I go to the kitchen for a bag, and I'm surprised to see a small, steaming pot of coffee on the stove, the heat turned low. The smell brings me back to my grandmother's house; the coffee was made very early in a little blackened pot, and it was kept on low heat so it wouldn't get cold. The same with the pan where the bread was toasted – when we were going to eat it we had to scrape off the burnt part with a knife.

My sister and I always said that was what had caused Aunt Vicky's cancer: the daily ingestion of that black crust, which you could never get rid of completely. Poor thing. In her final phase, Vicky had looked like a barren tree. Her arms and legs were bony branches. Her veins were blue lines, bulging and twisty. There was nothing left inside her; she was a marrowless bone. I knew all this thanks to my sister, who, oblivious to any notion of the respect a cadaver might deserve, had taken photos of her and sent them to me. I was shocked that I couldn't recognize Vicky: her features had sunken from the physical pain. Everything in her face conveyed suffering. She was naked, her pubic hair sticking up like a dense black mountain that contrasted with the paleness of her skin. Why had no one shaved her? I wanted to asked my sister but didn't dare. She wouldn't have listened anyway. She never said it directly, but I knew what she thought: taking care of Vicky and watching her die was more proof that she was a much better person than me. My sister was willing to be inconvenienced by other people's suffering. There'd been a couple of times when Catrina vomited up giant hairballs. Both times I'd thought of Vicky, dead, with that bush adorning the centre of her body.

I hear my mother open the sliding door and I rush to grab a garbage bag. When I go back outside, the rat is gone and my mom is sweeping the terrace in a big, baggy cotton robe through which I can see her bulky silhouette. Her hair is wet.

'Aren't you cold?' I step out and feel a sudden blast of heat.

'Did you have breakfast?' she asks as she sweeps a little pile of dirt into the dustpan and dumps it off the balcony.

'Don't do that,' I protest, 'the neighbours will complain.'

She wipes her hands on her haunches and heads inside to the kitchen with a determined demeanour I've never seen in her before.

'Go take a shower and I'll make you some eggs.'

'I don't have any eggs,' I murmur.

The heat is suffocating. In the bathroom I get undressed and into the shower, where I see a giant pair of knickers hanging from the tap, dripping. I pick them up, wring them out, and leave them on the counter so I can hang them up later on the terrace. I always take my clothes to the laundry room. In the closet I have a small rack that I used to set up on the terrace to dry my underwear, but since Catrina has been around my underwear tends to disappear. So I got in the habit of drying it on the radiators, which gives the apartment a trashy look that I'm ashamed of, even with my mother. I decide to go back to using the rack as long as she is here.

I stand for a while under the stream of warm water.

The buzzer goes, and I pray that my mother doesn't open. It must be Máximo coming to ask if I was able to get the box open. He's going to demand explanations that I don't have and don't feel like inventing. It goes again. I turn off the shower, rub myself dry, and go into the living room wrapped in the towel.

'Mami?'

I can't hear her. I put my eye to the peephole: it's the guy from next door. His wife is called Erika, but I can't remember his name.

'Yes?'

I see him lean closer to the door to talk, as if it were a microphone. His eyebrows are vaporous fuzz, his skin the kind that turns red just from eye contact. Nervous blond, prone to breakouts. A common phenotype in Argentina.

'Hi, I think the cat has turned up.'

'Oh, really? That's good.'

'Well, actually I haven't seen her yet.'

'Oh, no?'

It's awkward talking through the door.

'Could you open up for a minute?'

'Sorry, I'm in a towel, and I need to get to work.'

He steps away from the door and I can see his mortified red face, his blue shirt and sparse hair. The hallway light takes no prisoners. He's looking at a bag in his hand with an expression of disgust.

'Well,' he says, 'the thing is, we found something on our terrace and my wife says you threw it over. It's very unpleasant, and...'

I open the door. The neighbour jerks instinctively backward and apologizes. I peer into the bag swinging in his hand and a shiver runs through my body. I shake my head.

'It can't be.' I adjust the towel; the hallway is freezing, and he is silent. He's trying to look away but doesn't take his eyes off of me, because a female neighbour in a towel (almost any female neighbour) must be a regular part of a man's (almost any man's) fantasies.

'Everything OK?' Erika opens their apartment door. She has obviously been watching the whole conversation through the peephole.

'I did not throw that onto your terrace,' I tell her, and her husband falls all over himself in apologies and starts taking short, quick steps backwards, a gruff gesture that reminds me of a titi monkey. Erika keeps looking at me until he reaches the door, turns around, and slinks away. I'm closing my own door when she blurts out:

'I saw you.'

'So?' My boss is drinking mate. He looks too relaxed. Maybe he smoked something. Or had sex that morning. He once told me: 'Try to have sex on Mondays, so you'll be more relaxed when you come in.'

His name is written on a tag on his shirt pocket – 'Eloy', my boss is called Eloy – although it's not actually a name tag, it's marker on masking tape that everyone puts on their chests whenever there's a client meeting: that way they don't waste time on introductions. There's no meeting today, but when the secretary saw him going into the conference room, she assumed she should bring the tape and stick his name on his shirt with a couple of delicate pats. She also assumed she should bring in a pile of croissants on a tray and place them right in the middle of the table. Eloy and I are in the conference room because a technician is in his office installing programs on his computer. The place is too big for two people.

'So, what?'

'Tell me how you're getting on.'

'Wouldn't you rather go to the café? This is like talking in a stadium.'

'Café,' he laughs. 'When are you going to learn how to speak? In Argentina it's called a bar.' He reaches out and snatches a croissant.

I do a silent mental review: I say *café*, not *bar*. But I call the pavement a *vereda* and not *acera*. I still call the fridge a *nevera*, and not the Argentinian *heladera*. But I've started to call butter *manteca* like an Argentinian, instead of *mantequilla*. I still call beans *habichuelas*, not *chauchas* like they say here. But an artichoke is an *alcaucil* now, no longer *alcachofa*. 'You' is *tú*, never *vos*.

Eloy chews his croissant and juts his chin towards the tray:

'They're good, have one.'

I shake my head:

'I already had breakfast.'

Huevos pericos, pan de queso, café con leche, black-berry juice. I've got it all stored in my craw, like a turkey.

'OK,' he says with his mouth full. 'Go on.'

I look away towards the window. I can see the river.

I've worked for Eloy for two years now, and you might say we've built up a good rapport. Still, I know very little about his personal life. Some people at the agency think Eloy has issues. Like what? A secret file of abuse, they say: no one knows for sure, but when he gets mad he looks murderous. Absurd – in the right light, anyone will look like a murderer. And 'a little alcohol problem', they say that as well. It's not that he gets drunk during the work day or makes scenes at office events, it's just that sometimes he looks puffy when he comes in. Maybe he retains water, I said when someone maliciously mentioned it to me. No, they, his colleagues who see him every day, know more: they decide whether to talk to him or not based on the degree of swelling in his face every morning. They also criticize him because he slicks his hair back with gel for client presentations: 'Someone needs to let him know he's not Don Draper.' And so on – they say things behind his back, stifle laughter when he goes by, and he pretends not to notice. It's obvious to me that Eloy feels inferior. He is surrounded by young aesthetes, experts in demonstrating their superiority, even – or especially – with their boss. He has lived here for years, but he was born and raised in the countryside, in one of those rich, conventional, rustic families that Buenos Aires porteños hold in contempt. Once, one of the creatives – skinny, tattooed, androgynous – told me that Eloy wasn't always named Eloy. So what was his name, then? 'His name was Horacio, poor guy, can you even think of a less cool name?' His secretary blames his issues on his recent divorce: 'The poor thing just can't handle being cheated on.' In his office, there's a photograph of him and a little boy in ski suits. 'Is that your son?' I asked him once. He nodded and clarified: 'But I don't see him much.' I wasn't sure if he meant that not seeing him much made the kid less of a son. Or Eloy less of a father.

'What's up with you today?' he says, and finally swallows. 'You seem weird.'

I imagine that if I tell him my mom is at my house, he will also wonder how it's possible that after so long, he knows so little about me. Of course, if I did offer him that information, I wouldn't give him the complete story, I would just mention it in passing: 'My mom is visiting,' or, even better, 'My mom *dropped in* for a visit.' Even so, it doesn't seem appropriate. When people give us personal information in a work context we start to see them as a receptacle that must be filled with something, with more information. It's never enough, we always want to know more, we become insatiable: Oh, your mom? How old is she? How long is she staying? Do you get along with her? Better not tug on that thread. Best not to open the door.

'I'm still thinking,' I tell him. 'I'm not sure what you want me to write.'

Eloy no longer seems so relaxed.

'What haven't I made clear?'

'I didn't mean that, it's all clear.' I feel hot.

'OK.' He rests his palms on the table, trying to keep himself in check. 'Your job is to write a very short and appealing story about a cow who is happy because she lives free and eats grass and dies peacefully. Why? So her meat will be optimal.'

I nod:

'Yes, I understood.'

I just want to leave.

'Get inspired, enjoy the process, it's a nice job.'

When I think of my life in Buenos Aires, I do it in terms of casting: main characters, supporting cast. I think of a person who knows me and try to identify their complexities, their moral wrinkles. Usually I'm not sure and I assign them intuitively. Then I think about how the person would testify if I were on trial. What crime I'd be accused of, I'm not sure; I wonder if the crime itself really matters, or if anyone would be capable of defending me no matter what I did.

'OK,' I say.

If I were on trial, Eloy would waver.

'Great, kiddo.'

Every once in a while he calls me 'kiddo'. I guess it's a combination of paternalism and irritation.

'…and if you want to go back to that pasture place where they keep the cow,' he says, 'to see it or chat with it or whatever you want, go ahead. You already know where it is.'

'Got it.'

'Have you started yet?'

'Yeah.'

'Great.'

'Great.'

'OK then.' He pats the table with his hands. 'I'll expect it on Friday.'

'Friday?' I nod.

'How far have you got?'

He is holding back – I recognize his tone. He's afraid that if he pressures me I'll quit now that it's too late to assign the job to someone else. It happened once before and I'm not proud of it. It's just that sometimes I'm overcome by a feeling of lassitude that's so strong it becomes impossible to write a single sentence about anything: dried fruits, an art pamphlet, the meaning of life. Doesn't matter. Everything runs up against my sudden apathy and shatters. That time, after I'd missed Eloy's deadline for the job he'd assigned me – a very basic piece on purple corn flour – we'd talked about it at an agency party. A birthday, maybe. I tried my best to explain this defect that I felt as though it were a birthmark. I tried not to be self-indulgent, but neither did I fall on my sword and offer him my guts on a platter because, pedantic as it may sound, I felt I had the right to not be a trustworthy person. It was good to make that clear, even if it worked against my professional future: from now on you should be aware that assigning me a job includes the possibility that I'll quit halfway through. That was more or less how I put it. It was the closest I would come in this business to an outburst of dignity.

'I know very few people who are capable of saying that about themselves,' Eloy told me that day, holding a disposable cup of a young (that is, bitter) wine that a client had sent.

It's just that it didn't make sense to fool other people about something I didn't fool myself about, I explained. I suffered from the vice of introspection; in other words, I thought a lot about myself and drew a ton of conclusions. In other words, I knew myself well, and as a result, I didn't love myself enough to waste time defending myself: 'People who have a lot of self-love just haven't looked at themselves closely enough,' I said. It was an evening of aphorisms.

He replied that I would never be successful, that he'd read it in a book: successful people were not given to introspection. People like me, on the other hand, who spent a lot of time with their own thoughts, who were not very connected to the material world, would not prosper in any enterprise they embarked upon, no matter how insignificant. And that wasn't all: the book also said I would be incapable of surviving any kind of plague.

I sipped young wine from my own disposable cup. I nodded, though all that stuff about the book sounded like bunk to me. I imagined – as I had so many other times when a conversation reached a dead spot – that I was submerged in a warm ocean up to my neck, offering an empathetic and agreeable smile to those on shore, while under the water I was paddling furiously.

The party was emptying out and Eloy was still coming up with monotonous words, delaying the return to his solitary loft. I pictured him opening the door of his apartment to cross the threshold and enter a space where the atmospheric pressure was different from outside, more onerous and oppressive. Eloy would take off his coat and shoes and shuffle in his socks to the bar he'd had specially made – wood, glass, a lot of LEDs – and had shown us pictures of at an office meeting. Then he'd drop onto the sofa and get out his phone to google something predictable, like 'big tits', only to get bored and start staring out the window, waiting for the dawn. 'Sometimes I feel like my days are all the same,' he'd told me earlier, his words getting tangled up. And then he'd quoted a poem he'd seen in a Netflix movie: 'The sun goes up and down like a tired whore, the weather immobile like a broken limb while you just keep getting older.' And he thought that was enough of a preamble to try to kiss me, but I ducked, and he put his hands on my shoulders to keep from falling over. That was when I discovered that Eloy was one of those men without weight. A mystery of physics: he had bones, he had flesh and was of average height, but getting him off of me was like pushing a paper doll. He apologized. I told him: 'Take it easy, nothing happened.' And it was true. We never mentioned it again. It was nothing.

What did happen was that, from then on, warned of my unpredictability, Eloy made sure to chase me down about each assignment as if he were my therapeutic companion rather than my boss. Whenever he talked about me to a client or colleague, Eloy's mouth was full of praise but his eyes were flooded with alarm: be warned, the copywriter is good, but a little crazy.

'So,' Eloy asks again, 'How much do you have left to do?'
    I look out the window:
    'Not much.'

6

It's almost evening, and Axel calls. He says he got his hands on a massive fish in Chinatown, and he wants to make ceviche.

'Do you have ice?'

I go to the kitchen and open the freezer.

I wonder how I can talk to him about my mother.

'Nope.'

I open the fridge: it's overflowing with more food than it's ever held before.

I cannot talk to him about my mother.

'I'll buy some, then. I need to keep this little guy fresh, and I'm not so sure your refrigerator actually works.'

To talk to him about my mother I would have to go back to the beginning of time: chaos, darkness, the absence of language and meaning.

'OK.' I take the phone back to the sofa and sit down.

How can you talk without language?

Outside on the terrace, my mother is ironing. She's wearing black trousers and a flowered shirt that is very tight in back. She's tied a kerchief on her head that reminds me of when she was young, with black, unruly curls sticking out at the sides. Now her hair is straightened and dyed a shade somewhere between brown and red, like the colour of a squirrel. In the climate up there, you have to know how to mix hair dye. That sun is dangerous, it'll go to work on the chemicals like it's exacting a vicious punishment: it turns blond to green, chestnut to red, black to blue.

'…I mean, you never have anything but lukewarm water and melted butter.' Axel is still talking about my fridge. He gets pleasure out of denigrating my appliances, which he says are expensive and dumb. And that I have too many of them. It's true. It's also true that I hardly ever use them. That doesn't bother me, though – to me they are promises, and who among us doesn't need a few promises?

'You know what?' I say, 'I can't today.'

'You can't what?'

'I have to work.'

He is silent. It must be the first time I have declined his plans. We haven't been together long, but it's quite clear that he's the one who sets the operational agenda: what we do, when, where we sleep, what we eat. He seems secure in that role. It's a relief for me. I hate planning, I hate executing, and I hate the awareness that I'll never live up to my own expectations: all the plans I can remember coming up with to impress a partner have failed from the outset. I'm also relieved that Axel detected my lack of prowess in this area so swiftly, because it eliminated any temptation to fake it. So when Axel cooks, I grease the wheels: I make drinks, choose the music and the topic of conversation. I've figured out what subjects come most easily to us and which are less lively. So far, with Axel, the most efficient thing is to find the place where our desperation overlaps. Axel is annoyed by expressions of optimism, the way other people are bothered by complexity and negativity. Something similar is true for me, but I have more conviction because I'm alone. I don't have to pretend in front of anyone that deep down, I want the world to please me. The minutes I give every fortnight to the phone call with my sister are my only concession: I make her believe, incredible as it may seem, that this grey and silent life is my personal paradise. That I don't hope for anything more. Some days, it's true. The days I spend with Axel, for example. I'm moved by our everyday rituals. Sharing the capricious and the specific: I bought fish, I'll make ceviche for you, I'll mix drinks, I'll put out olives, do you like this song? When that's where the focus is, it's not that the world improves suddenly – of course it doesn't – but it does become more navigable.

'Are you there?' I ask him.

'Yeah. So,' he hesitates. 'I'll see you another day?'

I picture him in some corner of Chinatown with the bag of fish dripping close to his shoes and a small crack in his self-confidence.

'Sure.'

'If you want.'

'Yes, I do.'

'OK.'

And in that simple act, our relationship is tinged by something dense and inexplicable. It turns complicated. From that crack, something is going to grow and we don't yet know what it is. The view, shared up to now, that it is better to spend time together than apart has just been marred. Like when two children stop believing in a common fantasy – something that was just as real to them as it was invisible to everyone else. One of them catches on first and informs the other, and of course he wounds him, but it's not his fault. My friend Marah would have said it would be simpler to tell the truth. What truth? The only possible one: my house has been taken over, no one else can fit right now. There's her, she who is ironing on the terrace, and there's me, watching from inside; and there's that invisible bond that sometimes seems like an invention, sometimes like a warm embrace, other times like a straitjacket.

It's never night in the city – that must be the main difference with the countryside or the ocean or the desert. Landscapes with open horizons.

'The lights never go off, do they?' my mother notices it too.

'Never.'

We're sitting on the terrace drinking linden tea, bathed in the shade from the tree. They're called plátanos, I'd explained to her, which is the same name as our banana trees, but in fact they're plane trees that don't give you bananas or anything else, just the anxiety of watching them ceaselessly shed their leaves. For dinner we have pot roast with fried yucca and I have no idea where it came from. When I asked her she said: 'I brought it with me.'

'Oh. Really?'

'Of course.'

The heat doesn't let up. It's a strange autumn, so humid it makes my hair stick to my skull as if I'd doused it in oil. There's not enough of a breeze to bring any relief. My mom, though, looks glowingly healthy: she isn't sweating, which is very strange for someone who has spent her whole life suffering from a sort of undiagnosed hyperhidrosis.

'Aren't you hot?' I ask her.

She shakes her head.

Her eyes are fixed on the skeleton of the building under construction. I do the same thing sometimes: the structure, illuminated from the sides by powerful spotlights, looks like a work of art. I wonder if my mother might want to take a walk; it dawns on me that she hasn't left the apartment since she got here two days ago. She has been talking about tourist attractions, though. Asking where it was that people dance tango – I hate tango – and when she could visit 'the Monumental and the Bombonera' – football gives me a headache, and I never saw her watch a single match of anything – and if I could take some days off work to go to the south and watch the Perito Moreno glacier rupture. I explained that it wasn't something that happened whenever you felt like watching, there wasn't a button to detonate it, it ruptured every four years, or every two, depending on the weather. Between two and four years, that's what I'd heard. 'And when was the last time?' she'd asked. I had no idea. Maybe we'd get lucky and see it, she said. I started to get annoyed. I stopped answering and pretended to concentrate on the computer screen. I've never travelled in Argentina, I guess I was never interested, because it didn't even occur to me. Living here is an accident, I could just as well be anywhere else. My geographical location determines the mailing address for my sister's packages and not much more. Everything else – bills, correspondence, work – comes to my email. My only superpower, I once told Axel, is that I can do what I do in any studio apartment with good Wi-Fi on the planet. I'd moved many times without any great disruption. The secret was to live with the bare minimum, and avoid getting settled. Axel had squeezed me tight against his body: 'Wow,' he said, 'from here to there like a monarch butterfly.'

The thing is that my mom had mentioned those things, but when I said, 'let's go out', she grabbed a duster and changed the subject. And here we still are, locked in, prisoners of perplexity. Wasn't she supposed to be claustrophobic? She had been. Once, she'd stopped the car on Avenida Santander during rush hour and run to the waterfront gasping for air. My sister and I were stuck there, blowing giant bubbles of fuchsia-coloured gum. People yelled at us from the other cars. After a few desperate gulps of air my mother turned around and screamed: 'Motherfuckers! Can't you see I'm suffocating?'

'Why did you come here?' I ask.

She doesn't answer. When she gets offended, she goes silent.

'You want to go out for a walk?' I insist.

'I didn't come here for walks.'

She's more resentful than claustrophobic.

'Doesn't matter,' I say, 'Let's go.'

I get up from my chair and she follows. Inside, I grab the shawl I lent her on the first day and wrap it around her neck. We go outside and walk the first two blocks in silence. She looks at everything as if she had to write a report and didn't want to miss a single detail. I don't know what kinds of things inspire my mother's curiosity. I've learned almost nothing about her since I was eight, maybe nine years old, when my sister refused to ever go back to our mom's house on the beach. My memories of the rest of my childhood are few and diffuse. There was my grandmother and my aunt Victoria, always busy with something. It was astonishing how busy they were all the time, they never sat and never lay down, except at night to sleep. If one day a dagger had pierced their hearts, they would have kept on moving – setting the table, clearing the plates, mopping the patio – until they bled out. Then there were my many uncles, who swarmed around my grandmother's house asking for things: food, the newspaper, café con leche, polished shoes, the bottle of rum, a little radio that emitted some mind-numbing vallenatos. And then there was that shadow of doom always looming over us. I guess at some point I erased my memories to make room in my head for new ones.

Like when you need more shelf space in the closet so you throw out old clothes, even if they're in good shape. In sum, this woman is my mother, but I don't remember the feeling of being her daughter. And that gap in feeling isn't like the one left by forgotten songs – those come back out of nowhere one melancholic day, intense and complete. I don't know what to compare this feeling to, but every once in a while, a hologram of myself turns up to explain it to me. She shows me a dress I don't recognize, one that I find neither pretty nor ugly, though I wouldn't have chosen it for myself. The hologram tells me: 'You once loved this dress, you paid a fortune for it, you felt like a model every time you wore it.' And, after carefully analyzing it and seeing how innocuous it is, I have to ask: '*This* dress?'

We reach the park. It's not a good time for sitting on a bench. Maybe there is no good time for sitting on a bench in this park, or any other. Máximo says that the city is overrun by homeless people, their mattresses on the sidewalks. 'Zombies', he calls them, and when he sees one sleeping outside the building, he throws water with bleach on them and hides. Sometimes it's a whole family out there, and he still soaks them.

'It's pretty rough round here,' says my mom, and she rubs her arms again. I don't think I've seen that tic before either.

I look around: an obese woman and a small boy are digging through the trash.

'It's OK,' I say.

'Is this a good neighbourhood?'

I don't even bother to answer. There's a yawning expanse between her idea of a good neighbourhood and mine. The expression 'good neighbourhood', I think, is utterly foreign to me.

'How's the house?' I ask, but she ignores me and talks

about flowers. How I should have plants on my terrace, how flowers are good company.

'I don't know how to take care of anything,' I say.

'There are some flowers called forget-me-nots,' she goes on. 'They're lovely and easy to care for.'

'Are you still in the house?' I ask again.

'House,' she huffs. 'That's not a house, it's a torture device. Something goes wrong every day: the water pump breaks, the well dries up, there's a moth infestation, a mosquito infestation, a hog drowns inexplicably, the mule splits a hoof and we have to put her down. And on and on.'

'Right.'

'The other day they found an old man dead on the lot next door. I didn't even know there was anyone on the lot next door. I don't know what goes on around that house, I don't know what's outside because I'm hard-pressed to know what's inside.'

'There's nothing outside.'

'It's like it's floating.'

I see the house hanging in a cloud: just like how I remember it.

'And no one sees me. People come in and out and don't see me.'

'Who comes in and out?'

'Must be because I'm old, and no one sees old people unless they do very strange things.'

'Like what?'

'I don't do anything. I'm just there, nice and quiet, hearing those sounds that come from other places, I don't know where.'

'Sounds?' I think about the rumble of the ocean. In my case it never went away. Some nights I dream that the waves take the shape of a lion that eats the house, the lot, the plants, the animals, the jeep, the wheelbarrows, and everything it finds between the beach and the highway.

'I don't know. Sometimes I'll hear falling dominos hitting the table, and shouting, the way those bums with nothing to lose will shout.'

The same man from the other day is approaching. My body tenses up.

'Cigarette!' he shouts.

My mother jumps up and walks away.

'Hey woman, gimme a smoke!' screams the man, and she tries to speed up, but her feet get tangled and she falls face first on the pavement: her nose smashed.

I rush to her side, help her up and lead her to a bench where she can sit down. She's not crying, she doesn't complain, but her nose is pouring blood and I don't know how to stop it. The guy walks on past us, whispering things I don't understand.

'Fucking wacko,' I say in a low voice.

I use the shawl to clean her up, pressing the cloth against her nose to stem the blood, but all I do is spread it around, smear it all over. Her face turns dark, wet and shining. Only the brown iris in the yellowish white stands out. I stare at her, waiting for her to react. She gets up from the bench and walks, wiping at her face.

'Are you OK?' I follow her.

'Let's go, let's go.' She's walking fast, as if someone were chasing her.

I take her arm, which is freezing, and guide her to the building. I pray we don't run into anyone and we don't. Upstairs, I put iodine on the wound and gauze on the bridge of her nose where it's swollen around the scrape. It doesn't look so bad now; it was the blood that scared me.

She goes into the bathroom.

I put the bloody shawl in the kitchen sink to soak in water and detergent. It forms a brown foam that turns my stomach, and I run to the laundry room. I trip over the panels of the disassembled box and scrape my arms, forcing my way into the space between the laundry sink and the wall the panels are leaning against. I vomit. I turn on the tap, clean myself up, and go to the living room, where I sit on the sofa to wait for her. I press the button on the floor lamp with my foot, but it doesn't turn on: it's broken, I keep forgetting. For years, I've done the same thing when it gets dark: go into the living room, sit on the sofa, step on the lamp's button, which is round and large and gold and when I pick up my foot, it makes a sound like a tongue clicking against a palate. I don't like the overhead light, I'd rather stay in the dark. The street light shines in through the window.

How quickly the shell of a routine is shattered.

Any routine, however solid it may be, is obliterated by the unexpected.

It's strange to have lost that moment of turning on the lamp with my foot, and it's strange that it's so hard to get it back. For several days, out of inertia, I'll continue stepping on the button only to find, once again, that the lamp doesn't work. And every time I do it I'll say to myself: 'I have to go to the hardware store to buy a new bulb,' but I won't do it. The repetition of that lapse will be my new routine.

Outside, the moon is still shining; it's got smaller since yesterday.

Waning, we're in a waning moon, though that doesn't mean anything to me.

My mom takes a long time. I want her to come out, and I don't want her to come out.

I have the feeling that every passing second brings me closer to something I don't want to be close to. And it's not her, not exactly, it's what she came with. What did she come with? Aside from heavy food and popular tourist information, what else did she bring?

The wind shakes the window, and there's a screeching sound.

Ghost claws on the glass.

I get up and knock on the bathroom door:

'Are you OK?'

'Coming.'

When she comes out she looks like a new person. She's washed her face, combed her hair, and put on a big nightgown printed with watermelons. Her cut is no longer covered by my clumsy bandage, but by one of the small Band-Aids I keep in the medicine cabinet. The task of putting it on must have required a delicacy her nervous hands weren't made for, and I'm disconcerted. She opens the closet, takes out a bottle of passionflower tincture, and asks me for a spoon. I go to the kitchen, and when I come back she is in bed ready to sleep. She's put her hair up in a head-dress: a helmet of hair held in silver clips, like screws that keep her head from opening up. On top she's tied a red scarf. She sits up to take four spoonfuls of passionflower. With the last, she says something I don't catch.

'What's that?'

'I said, I came here to tell you something,' she replies in a scratchy voice. 'But I don't know where to start.'

She lays her head on the pillow. I turn off the light on the night stand. Before leaving, I carefully open the closet and take out a t-shirt, then close the door. I hear the intercom buzz.

'Yes?'

It's Máximo. He'd been taking out the garbage and saw drops of fresh blood in the hallway. Am I OK, he asks, since the elevator was on seven and Erika and Tomás were out, so it was just me, so the blood had to be mine. Am I OK, he asks again. The call really annoys me. The line between concern and nosiness is never clear with anyone in general, but with doormen it doesn't exist.

'Yes, I'm fine, I don't know what blood you're talking about, I haven't gone out at all.'

I hang up before he can answer. I take off my clothes and put on the t-shirt, then get my computer and lie on the sofa. I search for photos of Idris Elba, another way of escaping. But then I see Catrina on the terrace and go out to welcome her. I pick her up, hug her, pet her belly while she purrs.

'Enough coming and going like a ghost,' I tell her.

The phone, now it's the phone ringing.

I return to the sofa, and Catrina curls up beside me. It's Axel, wanting to know what I had for dinner.

'Lukewarm water,' I tell him.

He laughs. I ask him how the fish was.

'I threw it in the garbage: it was a party for the cats on my block.'

Under her fur, Catrina's belly feels cold and taut.

I sigh and don't say anything. Axel doesn't either. It feels weird that, for tonight, he's so far out of my reach.

'So what did you have for dinner?' It occurs to me that he had pizza and I say: 'Pizza?'

'Pizza,' he says.

I smile. I tell myself that I've known him forever. That there is nothing I don't know about him or that he doesn't know about me. That the story of our relationship is already written down in a notebook somewhere, and will therefore remain a silenced story until someone opens the notebook and reads it aloud. But who would want to do that? Not me. What I *would* want is to find out the end without having to go through the arc, all the stuff in the middle. Without hanging up, I open my notes file on the laptop and write: 'Every story is damaged in the telling.'

'Did you make progress on your work?' Axel asks. In the depths of his voice I catch a hint of distrust.

'No.'
'That sucks.'
'But something good happened.'
'Oh yeah? What?'
'Catrina came back.'
'Who's Catrina?'

7

The day Eloy told me about my latest work assignment, he said: 'I need a composition on... *the cow.*' And he burst out laughing. I didn't get the joke. Later I found out that the assignment was the local version of 'what I did over summer vacation' – yes, Argentinian kids write about cows. It doesn't matter how many years you spend in a place, doesn't matter how much your accent has adapted, or your vocabulary: if you don't understand the jokes then, you don't speak the language, you don't get the code, you don't belong. And the next phase is even worse, when you understand the jokes by dint of repetition, or through basic deduction, but you don't think they're funny. In a room full of laughter, you're the only one frowning.

That's how it was, exactly, the day of the assignment. We met in Eloy's office, the marketing guy, the art director, and me. All with our first names written on tape stuck to our chests. We were going to meet the creative director the clients wanted for the campaign: a photographer who also made documentaries and whose work was the antithesis of publicity, explained Eloy. He probably wouldn't accept the job. Eloy didn't hide his contempt for the guy. When I'd come into his office that morning he was telling the others: 'No one here is going to beg him. Who does he think he is? Who exactly has he beaten to get where he is?' But as soon as the photographer arrived, Eloy got up from his desk and hugged him like a dear friend on New Year's Eve. Then he introduced him with a little bow: 'Here he is, guys, Axel Haider, a real talent.'

Ten days later Axel asked me out, and he told me he had endured the torture of that meeting just for me. The first time he glanced at me it was because I looked pretty ridiculous with that tape running across from one shoulder to the other, like a rod holding me upright and keeping me from collapsing. My name is really long. His, very short. His tape only took up a fraction of the pocket where he kept a notebook and a pencil. The second time he looked at me it was because he thought it was funny I didn't understand the joke about the cow. And from then on, he told me, he was no longer interested in looking at anything else. 'But why did you even go to that meeting?' I asked him. He told me he always kind of liked going places he wouldn't have chosen, just to make sure he still wouldn't choose them. I thought: he feels superior, but he's also insecure. Otherwise he wouldn't bother to waste a whole morning on a useless meeting. Both things were confirmed over the following days, but they didn't bother me, they just increased my curiosity. Rejecting that job meant turning down a lot of money. Axel wasn't rich: Eloy's project would have kept him afloat for a good while. When I mentioned it, he told me that was all a big lie. What was? Selling your time to buy more time, he said. It was an impossible equation: 'Time is a kidney. If you wear it out, it doesn't grow back.'

That was almost three months ago, but now, sitting on the terrace with my mother – again, like a new old habit – the immediate past feels remote. It seems like all of that happened to someone else in another time. This morning, my mom has the face of a boxer; she woke up more swollen than yesterday. The bruise took the night to decide on a colour: dark brown in the centre, green on the edges. It doesn't hurt, she says, though she accepted two painkillers when I insisted. We had breakfast outside, then she swept and mopped (she's determined to do those things), and afterwards she got obsessed with my fingernails: 'Some cannibal's been gnawing at your fingers, dear.' She produced a pouch I thought I'd lost. One of those toiletry bags made of soft, flowered cloth with several pockets. Inside were nail clippers, tweezers, a nail file, cuticle cream, and the dark blue polish I used throughout almost my whole adolescence. She brought a bowl with warm water and sat beside me to give me a 'manicure'. That's what she called it and it sounded very strange. Up there, in her land – which is also mine – you say 'do your hands' or 'do your nails'. As if it were a magical or esoteric thing. You don't have hands or nails until someone comes and does them for you. My mother isn't very skilled; there was pain and blood. But I didn't stop her – her good intentions were endearing. The polish was dried out and she added some drops of thinner. She worked patiently. The result was grotesque: my meagre nails dunked in puddles of dark paint. I reached my hands out in front of me to get a good look. Each finger looked like it was crowned with an insect. 'How do they look?' she asked.

'Divine,' I replied.

When she finished she went to make two cups of herbal tea and I got out my laptop. She came back to the terrace with two steaming mugs and asked what it was I was writing. I told her about the agency's assignment, but I had the impression she didn't understand what I was talking about. The first time I told my sister about my job she didn't understand either, but she did consider it significant: 'If you didn't exist, I would never know that the labels on cans are chock-full of lies.' All because I told her they'd tasked me with writing raves about some bland lentils that were, in my opinion, pretty toxic.

'So, do you like it?' my mother asks, referring, I guess, to the job I've just told her about. I shrug:

'It pays well and I'm good at it, and there's not much effort involved.'

Or a contract, or social security, or transparency.

She nods and looks into her mug.

'But it's not what I want to do,' I say. 'I want to write other things.'

'What things?'

'A novel, I think.'

My mother sips her tea, nods again.

I see myself as a supporting actress who's turned thirty and still hasn't had a meaningful role, so she fights her insecurity by announcing she has read philosophers.

'I used to like to write, too,' my mom says.

'Really?'

'Really. There was a time when I used to keep a diary. It was really tiny, bound in leather, and it came with a key,' she laughs.

'Do you still have it?'

'No way, that was ages ago.'

'You lost it?' My own indignant tone surprises me. She has lost bigger things than a diary: a husband, two daughters, maybe a house.

'I don't know.' She narrows her eyes as if searching for the invisible shelf where she put it the last time. Then she shakes her head.

'Did anyone ever read it?' I ask.

She laughs again.

'I sure hope not!'

Keeping a diary strikes me as the opposite of having a child: it's a depository of secrets. A hiding place. A diary can keep the unspeakable locked away. Store dark versions of the world safely out of sight. Unless it's a diary that is sick with questions and fears and inconclusive sentences. In that case, it would be exactly the same as a child.

My mother gets up from the table and looks over the balcony, and I follow her.

I remember the yard full of trees, a table in the shade full of men, dominos, and glasses of rum in easy reach. And the salad of green mango with salt and lemon to make the drinks go down easy. My aunt made the salad while she taught my sister and me how to slice the fruit, lay it on the plate, season it. The amount of salt she used seemed planned to obstruct the arteries of all those men in flowered Bermudas whom we waited on like pharaohs – or invalids. My uncles, their friends, their friends' friends. Every time we went to the table to bring them something, we brought back crumbs of their conversation, which I remember as poor and lacking in jokes, but generous in laughter. And fights: the sessions always ended in shouting, and my aunt had to ask Eusebio to help her calm the gentlemen down. He did, and the threat of blows became a convoluted murmur that gradually faded as the afternoon filled with mosquitos and fireflies and varicose eyes. The revelation of this memory is that I think I see my mother sitting a little way off from the group: writing something in a notebook, or, I think now, in her diary. But it's possible that it's not a memory but a fantasy. Sometimes it's hard to tell the difference.

I see someone in the apartment of the couple and their baby. A neighbour who went to water the plants, I think. I wait for him to appear again, but he doesn't. It must be a shadow, then, a reflection. Everything remains still. Maybe he's hiding, watching us, taking notes on the magnetic notepad where the couple write down their shopping lists: two women with their elbows resting on a balcony railing, apparently deep in thought. Neither opens her mouth, though it's obvious that they are talking in silence, which isn't the same as talking to themselves. The conversation in their heads includes the other and it flows, but it lacks questions, and therefore answers, too.

'So what did you write in your diary?'

'Nonsense.'

'I would have liked to read it.'

'Nothing but nonsense.'

There is a version of my mother – and of me? – in a lost book. It seems unfair that I can't get to know that person. I feel cheated. I wonder who my mother was when she was writing her diary. Who my mother was before she was my mother. And after? I console myself thinking how the truth about a person has very little to do with what they write about themselves. Though many people think that when you write you strip down, I know that in reality you put on a disguise. You put on other faces, remake yourself in a way that blends guilt, frustration, and desire, and the result is a perfectly naked and honest character. And there's no real solidity in that. Such a construction can only be drawn on paper.

My mom says she's going to get 'a little something sweet'. I stay by the railing and see my neighbour the nurse pull up in a taxi. Susan, I think that's her name. León is with her, all dressed for football. His mom pays the driver, grabs his hand, and walks briskly towards the building, which means León is practically dragged behind her. Before reaching the door, the boy passes a pile of dry leaves that Máximo must have made that morning: he kicks it and the leaves scatter. He's mad at his mom. Why?

Over something like this: he wanted to buy a chocolate bar after practice and she told him that chocolate gives you cavities, and anyway, she didn't have the money. The boy would have let out a snort or a bad word that she reprimanded by grabbing his face the way I once saw her do: pressing her thumb and middle finger into his cheeks so his lips stuck out like a duck bill that intensified his look of anger and must have also stoked hers, because that time, the time I watched her do that in the hallway of the building, she looked at him with rage and said: 'I brought you into this world and I'll take you out of it.'

My mother has been in the kitchen all afternoon, cooking food for the week. At the table on the terrace, I made a little progress with the agency job. But very soon I took a break and opened the scholarship file. It's still raw. I'm still dumb.

I go inside wanting water, or tea. A cookie, maybe.

I peer into the kitchen and find the space transformed. Again, there are dishes I don't recognize, and dishtowels printed with fruits, a vase with yellow daisies, steaming broths in little golden pots that tremble on the stovetop burners. The pots produce a clinking sound like the laughter of children in horror movies, or the rattle of a snake, or the cowbells of a crazed herd.

The little kitchen has something hostile about it, as if it didn't like being handled. Really, the whole apartment feels hostile, like it resents being forced to transform into an unfamiliar creature. I don't recognize things, and worse, I feel like things don't recognize me. Every time I leave the house – to buy vegetables, run to the kiosk, take out the trash – I come back to find something new and disconcerting: clay cups lined up on the bookshelf, plastic flowers on the nightstand, a statue of the Virgin of

Carmen with a splintered nose, magnets of black women on the freezer with dresses that glow in the dark, incense smouldering in a corner – the metal stem stuck into a potato slice, since there's no incense burner – giving off a smell that stuns me and lays me out on the sofa in an incomprehensible nap.

My mother's use of space perturbs me, but isn't enough to make me angry. My annoyance is shot through with a sudden feeling of compassion that stops me from getting out the broom and smashing it all.

That time I visited my sister, when I saw the display she made of her kitchen, I thought more or less the same thing I think now: that most people replace what is lacking in their relationships with products. That is also the meaning of the packages she sends: I can't give you my comprehension or my company, so I'll turn what I don't have into a jelly roll, a hat, a crocheted case for your cell phone. Nor is this any revelation. It's knowledge that has always existed, and not just in my family: when there's a lack of understanding and people give up on ever reaching it through consensus (that is, through work), when incapacity or exhaustion win out, there is always food, gifts, objects that are deliberately unnecessary – and usually ugly.

I go back out to the terrace. In the end I don't get water or anything else. Catrina is outside. When I sit down, she climbs up on my lap and curls into a heavy ball.

I'm worried about not having a clear idea for the first part of the application. It's not very professional to apply for a grant with a non-existent writing project.

As I stare into space in search of I don't know what, I start to see snippets of things my sister used to tell me. It was so many years ago now that the details escape me. They were all made-up stories. My sister was sick of me asking questions she didn't know the answers to either. So she turned serious, sat down across from me and stared at me intently. And, like in a movie, she started to tell me the story of our parents. She changed the verb tense, narrating in the present, which struck me because it made everything she told me seem not just true, but immediate. 'What I'm telling you didn't happen in the past, it's happening right now': that's how I understood her stories.

She started like this:

Mommy and Daddy go to a party on a boat. There's a band, a full moon, and waiters who are serving whisky brought from La Guajira. The whisky is poisoned, and everyone who drinks it dies. That is, everyone at the party except for Mommy, who is pregnant and doesn't drink alcohol. That's how she is widowed and you are orphaned before you're born.

I don't believe you, I said.

And she rolled her eyes and said OK, here's the real story:

A ship, a party, the moon, the band – for some reason she framed everything in that scene, which she must have thought was romantic and tragic at the same time. Suddenly, a ferocious storm, surely a tentacle of El Niño – which was au courant in our era, but who knows about my parents' time – shakes the boat until it capsizes and everyone drowns except for Daddy, who's an expert in storms, because he's a soldier in the Marines.

A soldier?

A very brave soldier, that's right. But when he sees that his pregnant wife is dead, he starts drinking: he drinks all the whisky from the region, and he comes to a contaminated batch – brought from Guajira by native smugglers – and he dies of poisoning.

So, I die too?

No, you don't die. Miraculously, they take you out of Mommy's body and operate on you to revive you, but in order to save you they take me and drain all the blood out of my body, and they give it to you through some clear little tubes: long straws that they stick up your nose. Your baby body is tiny, but they still use all my blood. They empty me out, they don't leave me a single drop. When they give you to grandma the doctor says: 'This little girl was born thirsty like a vampire.'

What about you?

I die.

You die?

She nodded: Yep, I'm dead, I don't exist.

Then why do I see you?

Because you're full of my blood.

There were many variations, all of them disturbing. But I was grateful that my sister gave me something to hold onto. Her stories were my only cosmology. I guess they still are. With the rest of the family, our origin was always a locked chest.

I go back to the laptop, to the grant proposal.

Genre: novel (?).

Title: My Mother's Diary.

8

At around nine at night, the buzzer sounds. My mother is already in bed. I'm on the sofa with Catrina, nodding off to a TV show on the computer. I think it must be the couple from next door. Maybe Máximo told them I'm wounded. Or maybe they're coming to apologize for accusing me of throwing a dead rat onto their terrace: after talking about it at dinner, they came to the conclusion that it was crazy. 'Aren't we all civilized people here?' That's what she says at the building meetings when some discussion threatens to overflow the banks of the euphemism river. Erika chose smugness as a strategy for saying to the world: I am prepared to receive your blows before you even hit me. She speaks little at the meetings, but her eyes scan the faces of those present like she's looking at a dried-up garden. I detest her attitude, and at the same time I understand it. But it's not a rational comprehension. I feel about Erika the way I do about certain artworks that I don't understand, and as such I don't know whether they're exceptional or repulsive, but I stand in front of them and feel a sudden slap, and then the bafflement: why'd you hit me when I was only looking at you?

I walk towards the door. My plan is to face them with arms crossed, listen to her shower me in explanations, and watch him turn red. Both bodies silhouetted against the brown backdrop of the hallway separating our two front doors.

I look through the peephole: it's the nurse.

'Yes?' I say.

'I'm sorry to come by so late. It's Susan, León's mom.'

I open the door.

'Hi.'

'Hi.'

'Is León OK?'

She nods. I don't move; I don't want her to come in.

I want to take a machete and slash the floor to mark the line between the outside world and the inside one, and for that line to sprout a wall of fire that only I can cross. I lean against the doorway. Susan looks past me and sees Catrina:

'Oh, the kitty turned up.'

I sigh.

'Do you want to come in?'

'What's that smell?' asks Susan.

I ignore her. We're in the kitchen, and I pretend to be focused on lighting the burner under the kettle. The air is a hodgepodge of exotic smells. I can make out cardamom, cumin, clove, anise, a lot of coriander. The odd thing is that if Susan didn't mention it, I probably wouldn't notice the smell. That means I'm getting used to having my house – my life – stink of ultra-seasoned food. My mother makes raw materials disappear, takes the essential foodstuff and turns it into unrecognizable dishes. It's not her fault, not entirely. It's typical of my country's cuisine. You have to be psychic to guess what it is you're eating. It can be a delicacy, doesn't matter, but the origin, the starting point, is a mystery known only by the chef.

While the water boils, Susan looks at a shelf and sees a little bottle of rum that came in a previous package from my sister. It's almost full. When I pour her tea she gestures towards the bottle.

'May I?'

I nod. Susan pours a splash into her mug. It's dark, aged.

My sister believes white rum is for poor people and/or addicts and dark rum is for elegant and clear-thinking folks who every once in a while, after a complicated day, need some substance that will momentarily blind them, so they can then recover their crystalline view of things. I respect her reasoning, but I still don't like rum.

'You want some?' Susan offers.

Every once in a while, though, I give it another chance. I hold out my mug and she pours me a splash, staring at my fingernails all the while. A hideous sight. I examine hers: short, round tips, unpainted.

'Let's go outside,' I say, and head to the terrace to get some fresh air. She follows me. Catrina stays lying on my laptop, keeping watch over the closed bedroom door.

'I wanted to talk to you about something,' says Susan, sipping her tea. She's wearing a thin, baggy jacket with side pockets, and cotton trousers. They are worn, comfortable clothes. Her trainers are white Adidas, new, nice. I see, so that's what she invests in.

Susan and I have never talked about anything. The few times León stayed with me, she came to get him in the wee hours of the morning and carried him asleep back to her apartment after murmuring her thanks. She always wanted to pay me, but I refused. Once, she gave me a woven blanket, one with an aguayo pattern but factory-made.

I lean against the balcony. In the distance: the empty building in all its nocturnal splendour. Two more of her sips elapse, and one of mine. My tea is very bitter. It burns my throat first, then my stomach. It's as if I'd swallowed hot embers. A bubble of gas comes up my throat and escapes through my mouth in an embarrassing belch.

'I'm sorry,' I say. 'Something I had for dinner didn't sit well, excuse me…'

'It's OK, dear.'

Susan's eyes are shining. Is she going to cry? I'm worried. But it doesn't seem like a shine of sadness, more like contained anger. Something that surfaces suddenly and shows its hardness. A rock beneath the water.

'A little while ago, when León was falling asleep, I asked him who he wanted to watch him when I'm at work, and, well, he said you.'

'How nice.'

She looks at the floor, the ridges between the tiles spotted with moss.

I don't exert myself much cleaning the terrace, I leave it to the rain.

Susan looks up again. She stares at me but is silent, as if that gesture were a perfectly formulated question that I needed to answer.

'I can tell you're good with him, and I wanted to thank you for that,' she says.

'No, please, León's the best.'

'Well, even so.'

'OK.'

We are both quiet.

One, two, three sips of that horrendous but efficient brew.

'That bitch of a babysitter up and quit on me today,' she says. 'Can you believe it?'

I down the rest of the tea in one gulp. It's obvious what is coming.

'…first she told me she wanted more money, and I said OK, I'll find it somewhere; but then it's not money, it's a problem with scheduling.'

'She goes to night school, I think.'

I'm not trying to defend the babysitter, though I do like her because she's easy to get along with. I don't even know her name; every time she rang my buzzer she introduced herself as 'León's babysitter'. But she seems like a polite and patient girl. She operates diligently and without an ounce of disgust in the most arduous tasks, like wiping noses and backsides. What I mean is, she's proficient but cold. The few times we talked it was clear to me that she was working out of necessity, but that children were not her vocation. She didn't want kids, she'd told me once, right here on the terrace. That night, Susan was late and the babysitter wasn't going to make it to class because there was a transportation strike. She only found out after bringing León up to my place, and then I told her she could stick around too and we could have tea while León watched cartoons on my laptop. I didn't want kids either, I told her. Why not? she asked. Because I already have two jobs, I replied, one that I'm paid for, and another – the one that takes the most out of me and that I like the most – that I'm not. I couldn't work a third job, especially if it was for free. She seemed to think about it for a moment, nodding and holding her mug of tea. I talked to her about Virginia Woolf, to cite an authoritative voice: she had written in 1929 that 'a woman must have five hundred pounds and a room of her own if she is to write fiction'. 'Uh,' said the babysitter, 'almost a hundred years ago.' She added that with Argentina's historical inflation, it was better not to do the conversion. I thought that was funny, but it pushed me to do that difficult equation in my head: five hundred pounds, how many pesos would that have been in 1929? And you'd have to apply the inflation in Argentina over the past hundred years on top of that. Was that right?

'That's all a lie, that she goes to night school,' says Susan, and she looks at me suspiciously, as if having that piece of information situated me firmly in the enemy camp.

The babysitter's reasons were simpler than mine: a child entailed a long and very physical strain, and she didn't want to give her body or her time. 'Think about this,' she said: 'a person can only withstand forty-five units of pain, but in childbirth a woman endures about fifty-seven. That's like having twenty bones broken at the same time.' And what came after labour was even worse, she went on, because having a child required absolute and definitive dedication – if you didn't want to destroy the kid in the process, that is. Or lose it. Children got lost with surprising ease. Oh really? I asked, captivated by her categorical way of speaking. 'Historically, they've been the weak link: they're stolen, sold, dismembered,' she said. 'And no one defends them because they don't matter to anyone.' So you had to stay on top of kids all the time, take care of them, watch them until they could go off the leash, and humans took a whole lot longer than other species to get to that point. She knew it very well, she'd taken care of a little brother who had just turned fifteen, and it had only been five years since he'd been 'weaned', so to speak. Ten years, she'd given him. And now, to top it off, he was going around 'tempting fate' on a friend's motorcycle: 'a motorcycle, can you believe it?' She was terrified, but he was no longer her responsibility. There was nothing she wanted to give ten more years to, she said. And taking care of

León was temporary and limited. That's why she got so mad when Susan left her hanging and stole her time, it was just mean, both to her and to León.

'She's a bad seed, that kid.' Susan takes her phone from her pocket, types quickly on the screen and shows me. It's the babysitter's Instagram, and I almost don't recognize her. Her name is Flor, and she has black petals tattooed around her belly button. That's what I see in the photo Susan shows me now, as well as the start of her pubis – stretch marks, hair, bikini lines – and above, the creases of her breasts: two broad smiles. I envy that kind of boldness, the self-confidence some women have in displaying their attributes. Women who feel more comfortable than beautiful, and because of that they *are* beautiful. Flor is very beautiful. I am a sack of neurosis.

'What do you think of that?' insists Susan, indignant.

I think it's just great, is what I want to tell her.

'…and that's not even the worst photo she has, God help me.' She shakes her head.

Susan's accent throws me off.

'Where are you from?' I ask.

'The south,' she answers reluctantly.

The south is big. It's almost like pointing to a world map and saying: 'I live there.'

I think about the Perito Moreno glacier rupturing before my mother's astonished eyes.

'It's supposed to be beautiful there.'

Susan takes in air, seeming to evoke something she can't hold on to.

'Yeah, who knows.'

'Susan, I can't be León's babysitter,' I tell her.

She nods, returns to her tea and sips with her eyes closed as if it were a potion that would turn her into something else. Into something free and ephemeral: a dragonfly, a kite, origami art, a cigarette.

'How much do you think those apartments cost?' I ask, pointing towards the lofts. I want to move past that sticky spot. Susan opens her eyes.

'A lot. The building is almost empty because they can't sell them to anyone.'

'Really?'

'Well, yeah. Can't you see?'

'I can only really see this one, which is occupied.'

'Right, but in general, I mean. Can't you see how things are in this country?'

'Things' is a broad word, while 'this country' is a limited idea. I want to tell her that I have an enormous capacity to ignore everything that doesn't affect me directly: tsunamis, elections, strikes, macroeconomics. I don't say it because the statement is feeble and the argument would be tedious.

'You clearly don't get out much, chickadee.'

'Not so much.'

'Better that way.' She finishes her tea in two more sips. 'You're not missing anything.'

We both look straight ahead at the empty loft building.

I think of the collection of truncated projects: three floors of a law firm; two of an architecture studio; the consulting office of a psychologist to the stars; a spa that does hot stone therapy.

What is Susan thinking about? The corners of her mouth have their own gravity, and curve down involuntarily.

I hear a noise in my room, and I worry that we've woken my mother. Susan doesn't bat an eye.

'What time is it?' I ask.

She emerges from her trance and looks at her phone.

'Um, it's after ten-thirty.' And how she'd better get going because she has to fold clothes.

'Now?'

'Otherwise they pile up.'

Standing in the doorway, she looks at me: her dark eyes sunken in their sockets.

She's pale. Clearly, she doesn't get out much either.

'Thanks for the chat and the tea,' she says.

Must be the rum: I feel soft and generous. It's in those moments of weakness that the good me comes on the scene and butts in.

'Susan, if you have an emergency one of these days, I can watch León.'

'Idiot,' says the evil me, before breaking like porcelain on the floor.

Susan nods and smiles.

'Thanks.'

She's about to leave, but then turns back around:

'I'm going to give you a survival tip.' She wants to pay me back, and this 'tip' is her gift to me. 'When you feel overwhelmed, clean.' She grabs my forearm, and her fingers are cold. 'Organize everything you can: it's called productive leisure, and it'll be good for you because it's good for me, and deep down we're alike.'

Deep down where?

'…clean, until the weight of what you're carrying becomes manageable. Because it's not that the weight goes away, you know? That's important to understand.' She takes on a scientific tone that I attribute to her profession. 'The weight doesn't go away, it just gets lighter.'

When I close the door I think about the days I've spent organizing my clothes by colour. Single women are easy prey for 'survival tips'. I read in a magazine that a person's closet is a photograph of their psyche. From the test after the article I learned that my nature is chaotic. And what does that mean? Among other things: that I'm

85

not equipped for happiness, that if I want to achieve it I'll have to be diligent and work hard; and I should eat less red meat: when the body is heavy so is the mind, and discernment becomes more difficult. I don't know what magazine that was; I read it in the orthodontist's waiting room, and that day I believed it. I force myself to organize so as to pretend that I have control over something – this knowledge didn't come from any test – but the order doesn't last because it's circumstantial. Sometimes it's also preventive: I organize to keep from getting bored; that is, to keep from getting sad. I could have said all this to Susan. Saying these things is a way of keeping each other company. But I was ashamed. The idea that there is a body of knowledge that fits us all is naive. Same as finding a secret connection between someone else's life and our own. Every time someone comes out with an 'exactly the same thing happened to me', I know they're about to tell me something that has nothing to do with the original story. Maybe it's a gesture of solidarity and I'm incapable of perceiving it: to receive a second-hand anecdote and feel it as our own, and to transfer it to another person and then another, until the original story no longer matters.

9

'I can watch the child, if you want,' my mother says, as she picks up the tray from the wheeled end table I bought months ago but haven't used much. We're in the living room, where we've just finished a breakfast of café con leche and fried plantains with cheese.

How could she have heard my conversation with Susan?

I picture her with an ear pressed to my bedroom door, trying to decipher words and silences. I picture her pressing so hard she can hear the internal creaking of the particle board.

I ignore her offer, lean back on the sofa, and let her walk away.

I look at the table covered in crumbs. What a useless thing. It's so tiny that we had to put our mugs on the floor, and I was tense thinking I was going to kick them over any second. But really it was more hunger than concern; I ate with the voracity of a shrew. So we could be more comfortable, I'd got two chairs from the terrace and brought them inside. When I went out to get them I felt the drastic contrast between the cold outside and the heat inside.

Now, from the sofa, the view beyond the terrace is of fog settled on the horizon. The grey crests of buildings rise up like icebergs. Catrina isn't around, she's disappeared again. It's always like that: if my mom is here, the cat leaves.

'Poor woman,' my mother says from the kitchen, 'she's so sorrowful.'

Sorrowful is not a word of my mother's.

Down in the dumps, or in the pits, or knocked sideways. Those are my mother's kind of words.

She comes back to the living room drying her hands on a dirty dishcloth that she uses to brush the crumbs from the end table. She crosses my visual field: her dark shape is overlaid on the background of fog. All that remains of the blow to her face is a slight shadow over one cheekbone and eye; it's a floating island that has been sailing around the upper half of her face, coming to rest in different areas for a time.

'Have you heard from Eusebio?' My question comes out of nowhere. There's a name for that in neuroscience. Sometimes it's not a question, but a random sentence with no direct relationship to anything that's happening. They are often inappropriate words, sensitive, wounding. I think of a mutant whose eyes give off random electrical charges. These sentences self-generate like mushrooms in a region of the brain whose name I forget.

My mother shakes her head:

'Nothing.'

I see her go out to the terrace and, once again, throw her handful of crumbs off the balcony. Why does she do that? I want to grab her by the shoulders and explain a few things to her. What things? Thinking about it is exhausting. Organizing concepts, establishing categories: this is correct, this is incorrect. According to whom? According to the universal social ethic.

Years ago, my sister told me that Eusebio had destroyed part of the house. No one knew why: 'He walloped every door like he was fighting off Godzilla.'

When she comes back inside, my mother starts sweating. I think I'll have to ask Máximo to check the apartment's heating. What a pain to ask Máximo for anything. My mother is going to the kitchen to wash the dishes, she announces. I should get up and help her, I tell myself. But I stay right where I am.

Before, when we were having breakfast, I got a hot flush. I had to fan myself with my hands and take deep breaths. My mother looked at me and frowned: 'Are you OK?' I nodded. Then I looked into my mug to be sure she had made it right. It was right: more milk than coffee, that was how my sister and I drank it. My mom never drank milk, she said it curdled in her stomach. But her coffee today was just like mine: a *lágrima*, they call it here in Buenos Aires – only a teardrop of coffee.

When these random, topsy-turvy (another word of my mother's) questions or sentences emerge, I jot them down in a file on the computer because I suppose someday they'll come in handy. So I'm storing up a long list of gibberish.

'He must still be in the village,' my mom says.

Her voice reaches me filtered by the sound of water hitting the sink. I can just see the drops spattering the counter, the backsplash, the floor. Her presence is explosive. A description of her would not include adjectives like subtle, delicate, cautious, discreet, languid. Her adjectives are nervous, emphatic, fearful, clumsy, larger-than-life.

'…black folks do have a hard time leaving.'

Eusebio and his wife Machi (the only name I ever knew her by) must have been the most devoted people in my mother's life. They helped around the house, did the shopping, administered the property. But my grandmother disapproved of my mother raising us like free-roaming little animals on that banana farm, in the care of two souls who were good but wild. So she decided that we'd be better off with my aunt Victoria, at least during the week, and that we would go to a good school. We would trade in our smocks for some stifling plaid jumpers. On Saturdays, if we wanted, we could go back to the countryside to skip stones or stab sticks into the marine creatures that came to the beach to die. Why did they go there and not somewhere else? I asked Machi one day. She, my sister, and I were sitting on the mossy sea wall that separated one beach from the next. Machi looked both ways: the wind was shrieking as if it were wounded, and it blew up a cloud of fine, irritating sand. Then she replied that there were no people on that beach, that was why they came there: 'No one likes to be looked at while they're dying, child.' My sister snorted. Machi and I turned to look at her, and then she said she was feeling hot and sticky, and that there were mosquitos and the smell of algae was giving her a headache that clouded her vision. So we left. On the way back, when Machi went a little ahead of us to remove rocks from the narrow path we were taking, my sister, sick with annoyance, told me:

'Machi is embarrassing, she's so ignorant.'

I get up from the sofa, stretch, and go into the kitchen.

'How old is he?' my mom asks as she washes dishes and piles them up in a tower on the counter. There are a lot of dirty dishes for a two-person breakfast. I get a clean dishtowel from a drawer and start to dry them.

'How old is who?'

I'm still thinking about Machi, about Eusebio. They always smelled of salt. Sometimes firewood, too.

'The neighbour's little boy.'

'Oh, León. He's six.'

'Tell her you'll take care of him, go on. I'll help you.'

I look at her, searching for something in her face that will allow me to recognize her.

She'll help me? She, who is completely unqualified to take care of children. It makes me mad and sad at the same time.

I have a collection of childhood accidents stored up in my body. Scars that attest to the fact that it's a miracle I'm alive. I fell out of tall trees, snapping thick branches with my skinny bones. I broke my clavicle, knocked out teeth; once, I hit my head so hard that for days afterwards I heard a high-pitched whine underneath all the other sounds. I have more X-rays than photographs from my childhood. But I liked being at that house, unrestrained and running wild. I suffered every Sunday when my aunt arrived, because I didn't want to leave. My aunt was a good person, but boring. She was like a formal boyfriend you have to return to after a passionate weekend with a beautiful, adventurous heroin addict. My aunt felt something similar when she came to pick us up: she peered at us warily, as if our features – so well-defined on Friday – had been erased in two days, and now it fell to her to redraw new ones that would stick this time. She almost always brought guests. She would rush to meet us with a haste that was inexplicable – that is, false – and she would introduce us in a solemn and comprehensive tone, as if we were things that, after thinking about it long and hard, she had decided to buy for herself. My sister didn't put up any resistance. I would go down to the beach and disappear for a while that was never long enough to worry anyone. If the ocean was rough I would stay on the shore, but I almost always got into the water and sank under with fear and excitement, thinking that some animal would come and attack me. Under there,

I imagined my mother surrounding them all without their realizing, splashing the perimeter with gasoline and lighting everyone on fire, and when I came up I would find a razed jungle with no bodies in sight. But no, when I came up what I saw was an opulent luncheon served on the good china reserved for guests. And my uncles already nearly drunk. And my grandmother poisoning herself with bug spray. My grandmother's yard wasn't like ours: she put so much weed killer on it that not a single bird sang, not a cicada, not a cricket. She considered it a triumph.

I don't remember much more about those meals.

I do remember what those meals taught me: families are ambushes. Flammable places.

'We're going out today,' I tell my mom.

'Oh, no, what for?'

'I don't know, doesn't matter.'

'What do you mean? Where are we going?'

'To ride the train, to get some air, to see cows.'

'What should I wear?'

'Something comfortable.'

The train is almost empty. That's not strange, because it's a toy train: it's for tourists, and the ticket costs three times that of an ordinary train, which covers the same route on a different track. This one is made of iron and wood, it's always clean, and you get on it at a quaint, pretty 19th-century station, where I stop to buy some water. There are only two other passengers in our car, a girl wearing headphones and a sleeping man. I give my mom the window seat so she can see better. Suddenly I feel responsible for the view, as if it were my job to set the stage for her. The trip is long, and bucolic compared to the view from my terrace. We see big houses with yellow gardens go by, lit in a way that makes me think someone out there is interested in rubbing the world's beauty in our faces.

My mom gets into it: I see her looking out the way I've seen her other times looking at another kind of beauty. Sad. My mother looks out sadly because I guess the world, beautiful as it may be, isn't enough for her. And that gap left by the world's insufficiency, by something missing that the world is incapable of giving her, is her sadness. Love and sadness, when they're that intense, must feel the same, in the lungs. They enter the body in anxious gulps of air, never enough.

What is my mother thinking about? Maybe my father. How long do the dead stay alive in the ones they leave behind?

I don't know what my mother is thinking about.

When she looks at me again and I see myself in her eyes, I imagine that my reflection doesn't come from outside, but from inside. That I'm the one on her mind, and it's for me that she suffers.

'I'm here,' I tell her. Because I see her go out through the window and I want to bring her back. She pans her eyes over me quickly, and then she's gone again. My presence does not convince her.

It's a repeated scene.

Back then, at the house on the beach, just when my mother turned towards the window and sank into the ocean and its roaring, my sister would tug on my arm, pull me out of the bedroom and then the house, and drag me towards my aunt's truck. Vicky was already in the driver's seat, impatient to get going, while Eusebio finished loading the bags of our clothes.

'Are you ready? Did you pack everything? Did you turn off the lights?' she would ask, all beleaguered. And me: no, no, no. Later, on the way home, she would complain: 'We can't go on like this.' My sister would nod with her severe, worried look, and I'd pretend to be asleep. I thought about my reflection in my mother's eyes, imagined that when she looked at me she saw herself, and when I looked at her I saw myself, but in her guise. Like two mirrors facing each other. 'Everything has a limit,' my aunt went on. And I knew, even with my eyes closed, that my sister was looking at me, studying my stifled reactions. What was everything? I was thinking. If everything was really Everything, it couldn't have a limit. That didn't make any sense.

10

The pasture where the campaign's cow lives is in Tigre. There's a caretaker, but he isn't here today. It didn't occur to me to call ahead and let him know we were coming, because the two times I visited the place the man was always there, like an invariable part of the landscape. I watched him lavish the cow with the ministrations afforded to a duchess: he bathed her, brushed her, used a warm hair dryer on her, he polished her teeth and her hooves.

My last visit was about ten days ago, when I went to see the food engineer, who was also the owner's daughter. She wanted to explain things that were too technical to use in my copy. After listing the animal's muscles and tendons, she told me all about a natural drug for putting the cows to sleep before they were killed; that way they never went to a traditional slaughterhouse, but would have a calm, easy death. Why? Because the stress of the slaughter damaged the meat. They wanted the potential consumer to feel close to their food, to know where it came from, how it lived, how it died, even its name if it had one. It was very important to know what we were putting in our mouths, she said: 'It's important to know that this cow was happy.'

The first time, Eloy had brought me. The client had called from the road to let him know he would be in Buenos Aires for a few hours, and he arranged to meet us at the pasture. The man lived in La Pampa, where his cattle ranch was. The pasture was a lot that he rented just for the cow, which had been moved there when they'd decided it would be the image of the organic beef brand they were launching. No one would ever taste its meat; whether it ate virgin grass or rotten rats was not only unknowable, but irrelevant.

While Eloy and I were waiting for the client in his car – the kind with a glass roof – a feeling of unreality came over me. I wondered who I would be if I were someone else, who Eloy would be in that new scenario, and what the two of us would be doing all alone under that blue, blue sky beyond the corral. Maybe it seemed like a waste to be there, stuffed into that fancy car with Eloy, and not someone for whom that blue, blue sky beyond the corral would take on meaning thanks to my company. And vice versa. 'Why the sighing?' Eloy asked me, and, perhaps because I felt exposed, I told him it didn't seem normal for a copywriter to go with her boss to meet a client, especially outside the office, unless the boss wanted something more from her than a brochure. 'Then why did you come?' he asked, visibly annoyed at my comment. The afternoon smelled of eucalyptus, though every once in a while there was a whiff of mud from the nearby river. 'I wanted some fresh air.'

And here we are, my mother and I: getting some fresh air by the locked gate. A couple of cows who are not my one are grazing further off. I clap my hands to see if the caretaker will appear, but he doesn't.

'OK, let's go.' My mother walks away from the paddock, down the same unpaved road taken by the taxi that had brought us here from the train station. I see her walk as though bouncing on short steps, buffering the weight of her body. She's rounded out. There are women who tend towards the spherical and others who tend towards a stick shape. My mother belongs to the former group, and it's very likely that I am also heading in that direction. Seen from the back like this, in her brown trousers, black coat, and slip-on shoes, she could be any woman walking down the street. What if I let her go? What if I let her walk off and disappear among the people in town? What if I hid and spied on her? When she found herself alone, she'd have to look for help. It's a good way to put the story she has of herself and her circumstances to the test. When a child gets lost, they go up to an adult and ask for their mother: they say everything they know about her. My mother would have to ask for me, give my description, and summarize in a few efficient lines who she is and why she's here, lost in a foreign country.

'Let's go to the river.' I catch up with her. 'It's close.'

We walk a few blocks that leave her panting, and we sit down at the end of a pier that looks out at an old, dilapidated rowing club. I hand her the bottle of water from my bag, and she drinks. I take a sip too.

'So what's so special about that cow?' she asks.

I think about it a little and conclude that there is nothing special. I mean, it's a beautiful cow by cow standards – white with black spots – but it does nothing extraordinary other than slowly chew a bunch of dark green grass in order to demonstrate that precisely for that reason, because of its natural diet, its appearance and taste are perfect (and 'real'). I explain that it grew up in a vast field, that it developed muscles from wandering at will, and that now its mission is to redeem its species. The cows of the future are similar to those of the past, they must live free and die peacefully to nourish new generations of humans who will be healthier, stronger, smarter than those who gorged themselves on feedlot cows; the cows of the future will swell up until they burst and spill out, soft, generous, and pink, onto the stainless steel counter where they will be dismembered, compressed, shrink-wrapped, and distributed to the world as a panacea of protein.

'I see,' she nods.

I imagine she has questions. For example, what's a feedlot? But she rules out the idea of asking me because she isn't really interested in the answer. I'm not either. Just as I'm not interested in bringing her to see the cow, or to ride the train. It's all an excuse to get out of the house and spend time with her. To air out my head and try to understand. I inhale, and the air smells of mud.

'The thing I like the most here is the sky,' I say.

'Oh, really?'

Yes. It seems like the Argentinian sky covers more surface than any other sky I've ever seen. Light blue prevails over all other shades. There's a reason they chose that flag, I think – because the colour's presence is overwhelming. I remember León practising his song for Flag Day at school: 'From the high plains to the south, from the blue sea to the mountaintops, whenever I look at the sky, I will see my flag'. León sang at the top of his lungs with a solemn hand placed on his chest, the way his teacher had taught him. I watched him from the Chesterfield, the glass door behind him, its view of the clouds seconding his words.

My mom sighs, closes her eyes when she inhales and opens them again with her exhale. She looks pleased to be there, beneath the blanket of sky blue and looking out at the brown river water. An exotic creature acclimatizing to a new habitat.

'The sun's going down.' She looks at the horizon

with narrowed eyes, concentrating on the swathe of orange light about to go out.

More people settle in on other piers to watch the sunset.

We are melancholic onlookers seeing off a ship, offering mute, sentimental words to those who are leaving: your irretrievable past will remain here, but you don't know that. Handkerchiefs in the breeze. If I were less given to naturalism, I might just improvise a description of this sunset in order to impress my mother, or to take this moment and freeze it: please – a weak voice from inside begs me – let this twilight be unlike any other.

When I was younger I had a hard time not acting on my impulses, but over the years I learned to tame them, and I got used to frustration. Better that way, because sometimes the impulse was something as ambitious as wanting the world to be other than what it was. But changing the world from a solitary corner required the kind of effort that paralyzed me. Supposedly, change that is set in motion individually only impacts reality if you put in a massive amount of daily work over an indefinite period of time. Like the way an ant works. This evening I no longer want to change the world, I just want to change something between the two of us. But I don't know how. I would have to start by clearing the terrain. I would have to find the bare land, and the questions within her, and then I'd have to simplify them.

The sun sinks down, and it seems to go more slowly than everything else. It seems to have its own time.

'I wouldn't have known what to do with you two,' my mother says.

'What?'

'I had you inside.' She grabs her belly with both hands, that lower part that looks like a belt of flesh, a tender cut about to be sliced. 'Then I took care of you. That's what I did: I used my body and I had you and I protected you. Like any wild animal.'

The mother runs along the beach, climbs up the embankment leading to the garden, leaps like a panther and lands in the clearing surrounded by banana, mango, and tamarind trees. She hikes up her robe, crouches down and expels one, two pups, without effort. She cuts the cord with her teeth, licks her young clean, and keeps running.

'But the time comes when that's not enough,' she goes on. 'People need things put into their heads.'

'What things?'

'I don't know what things. That's why I handed you off, so that someone who did know would put those things in your heads. In the long run, everyone does the same thing. You send the kids to school so someone else will do a job that is a mystery to you.'

I wonder if this is what she came for. It strikes me as a paltry, disappointing explanation: three sentences against twenty years, more or less.

'I can't remember a thing they taught me in school,' I say.

'They taught you to get things. That's good, you have to know how to get things, because that's what it's all about. I don't know how to get anything. Vicky did know, she was ambitious. A person needs to be ambitious. When you lose your ambition, people call you crazy.'

'Right.'

Then she cuts a chicken's throat, hangs it upside down from a tree so it spits out blood through its beak. She plucks it, cuts it up, washes each piece with salt water, and places them in a line on a stone table.

'You two grew up and knew things. I, on the other hand, kept doing the same things as always. I hung your clothes in the sun so they would be warm for you, I heated water for your baths in the morning to save you from the early cold, I cooked you food I thought was delicious... You were destined for higher concerns. To me, feeding you was my highest mission. But then you had opinions, you said that lard was bad, that chicken feet were garbage. I thought, maybe they're right. I told myself: 'Easy now, you live in a cave and those two, every time they come, bring you light.'

The daughters watch her from inside the house: one is eating a piece of bread, the other is braiding flowers into her hair.

'...and I thought: next time they come I'm going to say this, I'm going to do that; I'm going to wash their hair with coconut water and brush it, even if they don't want me to.' She laughs a childish laugh, as if she's just said something very inappropriate. 'Because when you left I always had the feeling that something was left undone. Understand?'

For Christmas, the mother empties a small lamb of its dark entrails. She oils the empty body and fills it with plums, rice, garlic cloves. She washes her arms of the dried blood, the rank fat, the crust of muck. In the trees there are little coloured lights. In the house there is a celebration.

I've been taking notes for the grant proposal.

I gave up on the diary idea. It feels forced to keep track of the time when things happen. It assumes that there is only one time, or that it moves in only one direction: forward, and nothing can break it. We don't know anything about time. Maybe it doesn't move forward, maybe it doesn't exist.

Now in my notes there's a character I call 'the mother'. But she's not my mother. She's a little like her, but she's not her. My mother didn't do those things. She sat and watched as others did them. She would even give the occasional astute instruction: 'The cut is vertical, in the direction of the bone.' Or: 'Take out the kidney so it doesn't turn bitter.' But she didn't put her hands into the meat, because she wasn't skilled. I don't remember what she was skilled at. Looking, maybe. She spent all her time looking.

I always thought that was my skill, too.

'…it was as if in the moment I couldn't think of what to say to you, and I only remembered later. Once you were gone. Everything is easy at a distance.' She sighs. 'Do you understand what I'm saying to you, child?'

I understand. It's not the Hodge conjecture.

'…but then you never came back.'

We are very close; I don't remember ever having been so close to her. Physically, I mean. She smells of rosehip. My family wasn't given to affection. We were respectful of distances, stingy with touch. When I started going to my friends' houses and saw the displays of hugs, kisses, and caresses, I looked away. Especially when we were at a pool – all my friends' houses had pools – and bodies touched too easily. I had the sensation that all of them – father, mother, siblings – were getting naked right in front of me and starting to fondle each other.

I think that if my sister were to catch sight of us from her cruise ship, she wouldn't believe her eyes. Though this nearness is, as always, a matter of perspective. To my sister, from her ship out at sea, we'd look as close together as the stars in the sky. But who doesn't know that the stars are separated by a black, empty void?

'Look,' says my mother, pointing to the horizon.

It's a red wound. The scar that forms between river and sky before night falls. We are looking at proof that the space between us can be filled with something other than vapour. Is that it? It's not bad. But since I am not sure we are looking at the same thing, I ask her:

'What am I looking at?'

'The world!' she replies, suddenly animated. 'Sometimes it's beautiful, right?'

11

My mom had been tired when we got home, and went to bed early. I called Axel and asked if I could come by, and he said yes.

Now I look at the bed, the bulky shape in the darkness, and try to guess what my mother is thinking about while she sleeps. What is there in the moment before falling into unconsciousness; what's there, just there, before the abyss. She's snoring.

I go into the bathroom trying to make as little noise as possible: I shower, wrap my hair in a warm towel, and sit on the toilet to remove the polish from my nails. It's hard to get off, especially in the creases between nail and skin. It takes forever.

At around ten I leave the apartment and take a taxi: it'll be about twenty minutes down Libertador, my eyes staring out at those forests that seem to get denser at night.

I remember how the day I met Axel, I googled his name. Not his full name, just his first, 'Axel', to find out what it meant. It has two meanings. The first one is biblical – it comes from the Hebrew Absalom, which means 'father of peace'. But in its literal translation it means 'axe of war'. How can it mean two such opposite things? I mentioned it to Marah, who usually has an answer for everything. She sat thinking for a while, and then said, in her aristocratic voice – that is, a couple of tones higher than a plebeian voice – 'you sure you googled it right?'

The time I've been dating Axel is almost the same as the time I've gone without seeing Marah. Maybe I'm reverting to that teenage tic of abandoning girlfriends for the boyfriend of the moment. Marah is one of those brilliant girls with difficult childhoods, but hers was more abstractly difficult than any case I've heard of before. Marah wasn't beaten or abused or even looked at wrong, she was just abandoned in a comfortable house full of books and cushions. Her mom travelled, her dad travelled, her mom's boyfriends and her dad's girlfriends travelled too. 'But where did they go?' I asked. I didn't want to know their destinations, but to understand the meaning of their travel: it was one thing to be a tourist, another to be a diplomat. Marah didn't bother to answer. That information had to be enough reason for me to accept her tendency to confuse all her relationships – with her psychiatrist, her colleagues, her acupuncturist, even me – with an opportunity to be cured and saved, and, if there was a sliver of possibility, to sate her appetite for torturous and ill-gotten sex. When Marah was orphaned – father: heart attack; mother: overdose – she spent entire nights crying on my sofa, and I thought it was disproportionate. She hadn't seen her parents in years. Thanks to the nurse who gave her the news about her father, she'd also learned that she hadn't even been the first person they'd called. And who was? Her mother, who was in rehab in Uruguay and died a few months later. Then her dad's girlfriend at the time; then his ex-girlfriend, then his business partner. When her father had to make a list of his next of kin, he put her in fifth place. 'Forget it, they were already dead,' I told her. And Marah stopped crying and nodded: 'You're right.' But after a while she looked at me with eyes so swollen it was as if she'd been beaten, and added: 'Your sensitivity is blocked like the plumbing of an old house.'

What would Marah think about my mother's visit? What would her diagnosis be?

Axel opens the door wearing an apron that's a little too small for him. Axel is big, not so much in height as in size. He's built like a gladiator. Or that's what it seems like to me. When I showed Marah his photo, she thought he was more of a caveman type. Whichever it was, I told her, I like it. 'I like big men,' was what I said. When the words came out of my mouth it felt like a discovery. I thought: I value Axel's physical attributes the same way I value a high-quality mattress over a cot. I find his body comfortable.

'You got here fast.' He gives me a kiss.

'There was no traffic.'

It smells good inside. Something is cooking. I can't get a look at what it is, because once I'm in the living room, Axel leads me to the sofa and we have sex. That sort of urgent sex that happens to us often, as if we had to get it out of our system, purge our organisms so we can go on to function as normal people. The last three times we'd seen each other had started the same way. Sex in his car, sex on my sofa, sex on his sofa. Risky sex, but why state the obvious? If you walk along the edge of a precipice, you don't stop to marvel at the view.

'What are you up to?' he asks me once we're dressed and sitting at the table, eating meat, potatoes, and salad.

'In what sense?'

'Whatever sense you want.'

'I'm working on that cow thing.'

'Making progress?'

'I guess so. What are you up to?'

'I'm working on whales.'

'What?'

I think I've heard him wrong.

'I'm going to film whales.'

His voice has the victorious tone of someone announcing he won a prize.

I have trouble swallowing. Suddenly the meat seems chewy, even though seconds ago it seemed like a perfect morsel.

'Oh, yeah?' I say.

'Yep.' He shrugs. 'It's for a big project, it's money.'

I wonder if Axel has told me about this project already and I forgot, or if this leaving all of a sudden is something that is allowed between us, even though we've never talked about it before – or precisely *because* we've never talked about it before.

'A documentary?'

Axel nods, hesitant.

The word documentary appears before my eyes like a neon sign in the morning, strident and painful.

'Something like that.'

I want to tell him I detest animal documentaries.

Instead, I chew and swallow.

I especially detest the people who make animal documentaries: they're convinced that the planet would be perfect if it were only inhabited by those creatures. They would make it a healthy and hopeful place, and not the exhausted muscle we humans have turned it into. How naive.

'So where are the whales?' I ask.

How arrogant.

'Depends when. In spring they're in Puerto Pirámides, in the south.'

Two seasons to go until spring. A lot of leaves still to fall.

When is he leaving? For how long?

I think about León kicking the pile of dry leaves: I see them fly up, land, and crunch like broken promises. I see Susan's face, always too shrouded by other thoughts to notice her son's antics.

Will I be able to visit Axel? It's a risky and premature question. I let it pass.

Marah says that the success of a relationship depends on the moment you make the decision to incinerate the romance: 'As soon as you see it coming, you have to dump a can of kerosene on it.' If you reach that point and you let the relationship continue, it's the same as pouring the kerosene over your own head. And then lighting the match. 'Self-immolation,' she instructed me one day when we were lying on my terrace beside the clothesline hung with wet clothes, watching a cloud crawl past like a giant amoeba: 'That's the scientific name for love.'

After dinner we moved to his bed, and now we're watching a series that we both find boring, though neither of us turns it off. Everyone in the series is beautiful, successful, white, educated, and rich, but they're sad. Every one of them, so sad. I detest sadness, it's so presumptuous. I'm more familiar with anger. It's easier for me to understand what goes on with Susan and León than with Marah. Or my mother.

And Axel? What's going on with Axel? What's going on with me?

I turn onto my side and he imitates me: we look straight at each other and it comes easily to us. Like an essential movement and not the kind of intimate odyssey most people can't sustain. I look at my reflection in his eyes until he closes them. We're lit by the wavering light of the TV. I like Axel a lot, but I'm afraid I'm not reading him right. Not because I've noticed anything confusing or illegible, but because I don't know him, and he doesn't know me. A desert of uncertainty lies between the two of us. What if he turns out to be mean and controlling? Or one of those guys who hit on waitresses? What if he leaves and doesn't come back? What if he leaves and comes back different?

It's always possible to read the same situation in the opposite way. The first morning I woke up with Axel, he told me he was happy I had 'appeared' in his life, because lately he'd been feeling fed up. I thought: 'Fed up with what?' But since I was also pretty fed up, I said: 'Me too.' When we looked at each other that time – from the same angle as just now – I'm sure we were both wondering if we were talking about the same thing.

'Do you know the legend of where whales came from?' I ask.

He opens his eyes, slowly.

'No.'

'The sea king's wife died giving birth to their son. The child cried from hunger, and the sea king went to ask the earth king for help. In exchange for corals and pearls, the earth king sent him a herd of cows that would give the boy milk. But most of the cows drowned in the sea, since they were heavy and didn't know how to swim or breathe underwater. Desperate, the sea king cut off their legs so they would weigh less, and made a hole in their backs so they could breathe. The few that survived grew fins to replace their legs, and they blew out the water they swallowed through the hole when they rose up to the surface.'

Axel laughs:

'Where'd you get that story?'

He closes his eyes again, and his smile stays fixed. His expression is that of someone remembering a joke or a happy moment. But after a few seconds, though his face doesn't change that much, he seems to be imitating happiness and not feeling it. I switch off the TV and turn over. He does the same. Our backs are touching now. I think of Diane Arbus's photo of Siamese foetuses. I shift away from him and look out the window. Outside, there's a golden tree that covers the façades across the street. By night it's a leafy curtain, by day it's a blinding flash.

My mom is sleeping in my bed, in this very position: her face to the window that looks out at the terrace, which now has the blinds drawn.

When I moved in I'd wanted to get rid of the blinds and put up white gauze curtains; I liked there to always be light coming in, and I liked the idea of getting up and seeing the sky without too much definition. 'Put something between the outside and inside, kid,' the real estate woman had urged me when she gave me the keys, 'something that will filter the view.' We were in my room looking out. Empty like that, the apartment was unsalvageably graceless. The sun ricocheted off the terrace, shone pitilessly through the window panes and over-illuminated the mediocre finishes inside, especially the white, rubbery gunk that built up where the walls met the baseboard. Except for the spruce floor, which was pretty well preserved, everything was third-rate: the kitchen and bathroom counters were 'imitation wood' Formica, and in some places it had come up to form air bubbles. The terrace tiles were the cheapest on the market, though by virtue of being red, they gave the sense that the builder had planned that distinctive detail in order to save the space from its grey destiny. I pictured an architect, a woman, hanging on to her aesthetic dignity by her teeth, carried away in the Home Centre aisle and capriciously choosing something snazzy: 'They may be cheap, but they're snazzy.' She would think that gesture was the same as taking a bullet that would have doomed her project to a completely vulgar existence. In the future, some resident like me would come into the apartment and think: It's horrible, but the terrace saves it.

'So what happened to the kid?' Axel is half-asleep.

I turn around and face his back.

He has a lovely back, soft and continuous like a salt flat, slightly raised at his shoulder blades. One night I asked him what he did to get skin like that. 'It's my diet,' he replied, accepting my compliment unabashedly. I thought: Axel is aware of his body and feels at home in it. What does that mean? I have no idea. Is it good or bad? No idea. But it wasn't always so, he told me that night. When he was younger he had zits, he said. On his face, his shoulders, his back. When someone greeted him with one of those slaps on the back, so fraternal, conspiratorial, masculine, they'd pop his zits and it hurt so bad it brought tears to his eyes. A doctor had told him to stop eating a certain kind of fat present in some common food that, luckily, were infrequent in his meals. And that way he became the oddity that is a man with impeccable porcelain skin. To Marah, an oxymoron. In our constant early conversations about Axel, she always had some contribution geared towards lowering my expectations; that is, towards saving me from the disappointment that sooner or later was going to hit me: 'A man is a rough thing you rub yourself against in order to grow softer, end of story!'

'What kid?' I ask.

'The sea king's son,' Axel murmurs.

'He lived and reigned.'

It's very late. I figure it's three, four in the morning.

I'm not sleepy anymore. I close my eyes and make up

a dream instead: around noon I say goodbye to Axel, get into a taxi and go back to my apartment. When I open the door I see Axel again, sitting on the Chesterfield and talking to my mom. They're laughing. 'Why didn't you tell me?' Axel asks, amused, but my mom answers first: 'There's nothing to tell.' She waves her hand. 'We're all here, we're all fine now.' 'Where's Catrina?' I ask, overcome by a horrible presentiment. I run to the terrace and peer over the balcony, and I see her broken on the pavement, her belly up and open, dozens of kittens crawling out of it.

'My god,' I open my eyes. 'Catrina.'

'Who?' Axel asks.

I don't answer.

12

It's after 12. Axel offers me a ride, but I decline.

'I want to get some air,' I say, and he puts his hands up as though saying: Don't let me come between the air and your nose.

We drank mate earlier; he offered me croissants, but I didn't want one. I ate a mandarin, he ate a banana and kiwi and a mix of seeds that his nutritionist had made for him. Finally he went for a croissant, which was a relief. I thought that if this was the last time I was going to see him, I didn't want to be left with the image of a guy who avoided carbs.

His plan for today is to go swimming.

Then he'll have a video call with the producers of the whale project. They're Swiss, or maybe Finnish. I wasn't listening when he told me. They'll set the dates during that meeting.

'Right.'

I look around his house: the grey sofa, the wooden steps that lead to the second floor, to his bedroom, his bathroom full of shampoos that smell citrusy; the tall windows with frosted glass; the ceiling lamps, white like the walls, which are oddly empty for the house of a photographer. The pictures he does have are leaning in a corner of the living room, one against the other, some still wrapped in plastic. It looks like they've just been moved in, or are about to be moved out. Most are gifts from colleagues. 'When I'm at home I like to rest my eyes,' he said when I asked about his bare walls. 'I need to cleanse my palate.'

I look at everything with the same curiosity I had the first time, because I have the feeling that this could be the last. If it is, I don't want to forget any details. Why not? So I have something to hold on to when I miss him, I think, in a fit of dramatics.

'When will I see you?' asks Axel, reaching out to push a lock of hair from my shoulder, as if he were preparing me for a portrait.

I wonder if he is doing the same thing with my face as I'm doing with his house. Memorizing it.

I imagine him getting out his camera and taking a picture that he then forgets about. But one day, clearing his memory cards, he finds me there, with eyes full of questions I never asked. Months could pass before he sees my face again. Can you forget a face in months? Not the whole thing, but details, yes. Retaining all the details is impossible, it's an attempt to encompass all the constellations of a galaxy. When he saw my face again he would recognize me, of course he would, but he'd be surprised by some feature or expression that perhaps he didn't pay attention to at the time. Then maybe he would find the key to whatever it was that didn't click, that he never fully understood, that kept him from staying with me instead of going off to film whales.

What's wrong with me? I think. Why doesn't he choose me?

'Soon,' I tell him.

'When?' he insists, cocking his head to the side.

I am a candle that burns out before the impassive gaze of another.

'I don't know.'

'Let's talk later?'

'OK.'

When I reach the building I see León sitting on the entrance steps. He looks bored, or angry. Most likely he can't decide, either, which of the two feelings bothers him more and is forcing him to curl in on himself like one of those plants that closes up when you touch it. The school bus driver is pacing up and down the sidewalk, phone to her ear. I figure she's talking to Susan; I hear her say that she can't wait that long, she has other kids to drop off.

'Hi,' León says to me.

'Hi,' I reply. 'What're you doing here?'

León shrugs diffidently.

What a stupid question. What could he be doing there? How could the poor kid answer that question? Just as he did: feigning disinterest.

The bus driver comes over to me.

'Hang on a second, and no need to get upset,' she says into the phone in a voice that wants to be soothing, but comes out harsh. 'There's a girl here talking to León.' She turns to me: 'Are you the babysitter?'

I hear Susan's voice coming from the phone, but I can't make out her words. The woman says: 'I'll put her on,' and hands me her phone.

In my apartment León shuffles off his backpack, his shoes, his coat and sweatshirt, as if shedding layers of skin as he walks. I follow him but don't pick up his things, I just watch as they fall to the floor. I wonder where my mother is. The bedroom door is open and everything is neat and clean. I check the kitchen, but it's empty. On my way back to the living room I accidentally step on León's sweatshirt, which was left twisted up on the floor like a grimace of fear. León is already settled in on the sofa with crossed legs, elbows resting on his knees, and chin in his hands. He huffs:

'You still don't have a TV?'

'No, but I have something better.' I open the sliding glass door and go out to the terrace, where Catrina is sleeping in the sun. León jumps up and follows me. He lunges at the cat like a greyhound on a hare, and Catrina tries to flee, but León is faster.

'You came back!' He hugs her so hard Catrina mews. Finally she gives up and lets the boy pet her, and he automatically recovers his good mood, as if his mother had never forgotten him on the pavement.

'I'm going to make some snacks.' I go inside.

I see my mom in the kitchen doorway. Her presence startles me. She has already cut slices of bread, put butter in the butter dish and taken out ham and cheese. There's also a plate with cubes of guava jelly. It's all set out on the counter.

'Wow,' I say.

She smiles at me. The bruise on her face has reappeared. How random, it comes and goes when it pleases. I have an irrepressible urge, and I reach out and touch it. I'm drawn to the taut skin on her cheekbone: stretched, shiny, and smooth like plastic. She doesn't move, lets me touch her; when my fingertips come in contact with her skin it's as if I were touching my own face, a slight pain in the bone that makes me blink. In that blinking of an eye, which lasts seconds, I'm swarmed by images that play out quickly but clearly.

My sister taking me by the shoulders, leading me away from that dark room that looked out at the sea and the storm, noisy like a round of applause. My sister and I sitting on a hollow log under banana and palm trees, the rubber tree that dripped sticky gobs of spit, and above it all, the moon: a shining brushstroke in the darkness. My sister and me blinded by the high beams of a truck that was driving up fast and honking the horn: 'Finally,' said my sister, squeezing my hand.

'She ran away!' León shouts from outside.

I start to go out and trip over him in the hall; he has both arms outstretched to show me the scratches.

'Let's clean you up.' I take him into the bathroom and wash his arms with soap and water.

'I didn't do anything to her,' he says. 'I petted her and she did this.'

'She gets mean sometimes.'

'But why?' he asks in a shaky voice. 'I didn't do anything to her.'

I use an antiseptic spray and he complains that it burns. I hand him some gauze:

'Wipe it off.'

He obeys in silence.

When we go back outside, the table is set. A sandwich cut in triangles, a bowl with cherry tomatoes, the little plate of guava jelly. León looks at it all with some confusion. My 'snacks' tend to be more austere. I tell him to sit down, that I'll get some water and be right back. But as I'm going inside, my mother comes out holding a glass of chocolate milk. We return to the terrace together and sit down. She sets the glass on the table, and León grabs it and chugs it down with gusto.

'This is my mom,' I tell him.

He stops drinking, looks at us, and laughs as if someone were tickling him diabolically. He returns to his glass and drinks in slow, continuous swigs. I look at my mom in bewilderment, because she is also laughing.

'What are you two laughing at?' I ask.

My mom raises her hands in a gesture of impotence as though saying, 'What do I know.'

Then Catrina appears, standing on the neighbours' dividing wall. She has something in her mouth that she drops to the ground with a dry, heavy thud: a fat, immense pigeon that is trembling in its death throes.

'Disgusting,' my mom says and hurries inside. I figure she's going to get a bag for the dead bird, but it takes her a while to come back.

'Don't move, don't touch it,' I tell León, and I head to the kitchen, where I get plastic gloves and a bag. 'Mom?' I call. No answer.

She's terrified of the cat, how absurd. Her house used to have snakes coiled on the floor of the shower. There was also a fox trapped in the attic that galloped all night from one end to the other – badadoom, badadoom, badadoom. 'It's the sound of the dead,' Machi told us when my sister, hands over her ears, asked her to please get Eusebio's shotgun and shoot it.

When I come outside, León is still at the table and Catrina is eating from his hand. She gobbles up a piece of guava jelly. I can't imagine it's going to sit well with her and I see myself later, cleaning up the vomit. The pigeon is gone.

'Where's the bird?' I ask León.

'I dunno.' He shrugs.

'A dead bird can't fly away, León. What did you do with it?'

I get mad. I feel my head heating up and I want to shake León and demand he give back the damned cadaver. He's already disrupted my day enough. I sigh and go over to the dividing wall, put my hands on it

120

and jump up to get a look at the other side. There it is. The pigeon, fat, dead, and bloody, dropped like a turd onto Erika's terrace. I curse everything. I have to get it out of there fast to avoid another uncomfortable conversation in the hallway. To avoid a complaint to the condo committee or a report to the municipality.

I get a chair, climb up, and clamber over to the other side, where I put on gloves so I can pick up the pigeon.

Now here, there are plants. Lots of them. Pretty ones. The windows have curtains with a pattern that's almost imperceptible, but that lends a romantic shading to everything beyond them. The living room and kitchen are a single large space. There's a bright striped rug, a long dining table with a marble top and natural wood chairs, maybe oak, with lemon yellow cushions, and framed children's drawings on the walls. A niece or nephew, I think. I go over to the bedroom window, press my face to the glass and shade my eyes with a hand to get a better look. The bed has a violet crocheted bedspread. The side tables have very nice reading lamps. I recognize them, they're Italian. I'm sure my neighbours brought them back from a trip, because you can't get those here. What do Erika and Tomás do? Four years living next door to them and I never thought about it. Their place is lovely. It doesn't resemble them much. The bathroom door opens and Erika appears: her anxious eyes looking into mine. I jerk impulsively backwards, run to the dividing wall, jump to the other side, and forget the pigeon.

13

The park is full of kids, nannies, and birds.

León didn't understand why we had to rush out so fast just to take a walk, but he didn't fight it. Now, here, he seems happy. He's been playing for a while with a ball that no one has come to claim. I'm hugging his backpack. Earlier, I opened it: there are two notebooks – one blue, another red – and a pencil case. Today he used the blue notebook. He wrote the date and the lesson for the day:

Transparent means light goes through.

Opaque means light can't go through.

Translucent means a little light goes through.

He has homework: find and classify objects according to those qualities.

I start to do it in my head: The window is transparent; the blinds are opaque; Erika's curtain is translucent.

It's a pretty park, in spite of the neglect. But kids don't see that, kids only see other kids, and they size one another up and approach and sniff each other like dogs in a plaza. Even if they don't have any other contact, if they don't even exchange words, there's something about just being around other kids that changes their mood and does them good.

My phone has vibrated four times. It's an unknown number and I don't answer. It could be Erika, Máximo, Susan. Or it could be my mother.

León kicks the ball far and runs after it, startling some birds into the air. I have to stand up and follow. He runs so fast that I'm forced to trot to catch up with him.

'Slower,' I say once I'm beside him.

He says OK, but doesn't slow down. He reaches the ball and keeps kicking it, now against a wall at the end of the park that has a painting of a giant spider against a rain of colours. I sit down on another bench where I have a view of León from behind and the spider head-on.

By now Axel must have a clear idea of the whale timeline. If he hasn't called to let me know it's because he doesn't feel a need to keep me in the loop. Just who do I think I am? The piece of meat he's been chewing these past few months – end of story. And him, who the hell does he think he is? All this time I've been so caught up feeling watched by Axel that I lost sight of him. It's possible that Axel was just staring into space. Our ability to fool ourselves is infinite. Suddenly I feel angry, hurt, betrayed, seduced like a virgin and dumped like a whore. I've been quick to anger lately. 'Lately' is a confusing period of time that encompasses several outbursts. Up until recently my life was a small vehicle that moved along a more or less safe track. Now it feels like a truck that could skid at any moment.

Eloy. It could also be Eloy calling. Tomorrow is my deadline for the copy on the happy cow.

'León!' I shout. The kid doesn't pay me the slightest attention. So I yell louder, and several heads turn panicked eyes my way. León walks towards me staring at the ground, embarrassed. Horrified, maybe. His steps are short but quick. I take him firmly by the hand and wonder if he really was the one who threw the dead pigeon over the wall. I had accused him without giving him a chance to defend himself. I'd wagged a finger and scolded him as if he weren't someone else's child, the child of someone with such a brittle sensibility. Then I'd rushed him to put his sweatshirt on and to get out of the apartment before Erika could leave hers. The elevator was on six, so we ran down a flight of stairs to catch it. We fled in silence, like criminals. Now I remember the surprise in León's eyes and I start to doubt.

If it wasn't him, it was my mother.

'Let's go, hurry,' I tell him now. 'We have to get back.'

Just like with the rat. But when? Why?

León murmurs something I don't catch.

'I can't hear you,' I tell him.

He repeats the incomprehensible words with his eyes still fixed on the ground, which infuriates me further. I curse Susan for putting me in this situation. I relive her hysterical pleas on the phone, her exasperated voice in my ear. I squeeze León's hand and walk faster. If you can't take care of your child, 'chickadee', don't have one.

'Let me go!' León shouts, and pulls away.

We're out of the park, waiting for the light to change so we can cross the street. I look at him. He's crying. His trousers have a wet urine stain that reaches down to his boot and drips onto the sidewalk.

'I told you, I told you,' he repeats, 'but you didn't listen.'

I kneel down and hug him tightly. I feel like crying with him, and that's what I do. We cling to one another, because there is no one else. We form a motionless lump that people dodge with annoyance, a mile-marker badly placed on a furious corner, a tight cyst in the city's disoriented circulation. Three poor metaphors that, on top of it all, weep with a grief that's disproportionate to the incident. I want to explain it all to León, how the good thing about crying is that it cleans out clogged-up sorrows that are never the ones of the moment, but others: we cry over what has happened and over what we don't even know is going to happen. And the harder we cry, the more powerful the current that carries it all away. That's why I don't hold back. The two of us cry wholeheartedly and without shame. We swallowed a river, and now we have to expel it to get the bad taste out of our mouths, to deflate and cure ourselves. The light changes three times before we are able to get up and keep going.

'I knocked at your door for a long time,' says Susan, her arms crossed accusatorially. 'I almost kicked it down.'

We are in her apartment. León went inside without greeting her, sat down on a faded sofa, and turned on the TV. Susan doesn't have a terrace, but her living room is bigger than mine. The place smells of disinfectant. There are a few decorations placed carelessly: a plastic Buddha, an empty napkin holder, the waving golden cat. There's a low table covered with bills, crayon nubs, and a teacup full of beer.

She was really scared, she says. Because I didn't answer the phone, or open the door; she even thought she heard noises coming from inside.

'It's the wind,' I tell her. 'We went out in a hurry and I left the windows open.'

Out of the corner of her eye she looks at León, engrossed in the screen. The stain is dry but visible.

'What's that on León's trousers?' she whispers. 'Is that…?'

She doesn't finish.

'I have to go,' I tell her.

'What are those scratches on his arms?' she continues.

I'm surprised that five seconds were enough for her

to scan her son in such detail. Just the outside, I think. Anyone can do that. Your son has Spanish homework, Susan: that's more than you know. I win. I want to tell her that the kid cried for ten minutes straight because she abandoned him with a stranger.

'The cat scratched him.' I head for the door. 'He can tell you about it.'

'But is everything OK?' she insists, grabbing my arm to keep me from leaving. I pull away, get mad. What does she mean, 'is everything OK?' How can she ask me that – *her*? Doesn't she have enough evidence to the contrary? I take a breath. I try to take in the full picture before me:

The scowl of continual annoyance on her face.

The black roots in her blond hair.

The rough, threadbare clothes.

Her eyes too sunken to bother reviving them.

The kid in the background, like a stain on her life.

'I have to go,' I repeat.

I rush out of the building to keep from running into Erika. I imagine her hunting me in the hallway, in the elevator, in the building lobby. I walk for several blocks, go into a bar and order a bottle of water. I only have a hundred-peso bill in my pocket. The water flows down my throat and skips all my other organs to go straight to my bladder. Now I need the bathroom. I go and sit down on the toilet. My urine has a strong smell, as if I'd eaten asparagus. No, it smells like passionflower. I ask for the bill and pay. I want to stay a while longer, but I'm ashamed of not consuming anything. I catch the disapproval in the other customers' eyes: here comes another immigrant to steal the heat. I leave.

When I first got here I did steal, and openly. I'd go into a cafe to warm up, and when the waiter came over I'd put my hands together and say: 'I don't have a cent, I'm cold, I'll leave in five minutes.' The plea was camouflaged by my friendly voice and by my appearance, which wasn't that of a hobo. So they'd let me stay and they'd often give me a hot drink, or a churro or croissant. 'Just cos you're cute,' a waiter said once, winking at me. Then he brought me a beer, a little plate of olives, and a napkin with his number on it. I saved it for months. Now *he* was cute. Very. But I never called him. One of the glitches left by my upbringing was the impossibility of mixing with the working class. That waiter had a better income and better genes than I did – according to the criteria that underlie my childhood glitches – but he was a waiter. On an impulse, to make him more palatable, I had asked him if he studied or did something else besides clean tables – yeah, sure, I make paintings, sculptures, poetry, gadgetry, software, documentaries, cochlear implants –. But no, nothing, this was his full-time job – his tone was victorious – but he had Fridays off. And he winked at me again.

I walk towards the building, but I don't want to be there. I sit down on a bench and think about how I've been here before. Not on this bench, but in this fix. The fix of futility. I look at myself from outside and it's like sitting in front of a life I already lived. I recognize everything, but there is no nostalgia. Only irritation. And I feel a rope attached to my back and pulling on me. It's not going to take me to any paradise, I know, because I've let myself be dragged along on other occasions. The rope is the desire to escape from what I know, the desire to lose myself. But the person I am eventually catches up with me, because she differs from my impulses. And what does she do? She pulls on the rope in the opposite direction and stamps me down here again, on this bench.

I regret so many things that their mere enumeration solidifies behind my forehead and keeps me from thinking. I regret accepting the job on the cow, I regret committing to apply for the grant, I regret allowing myself to be saddled with a necrophiliac cat. I regret meeting Axel, I regret falling in love with Axel. I regret not being unequivocal with Susan: you two won't fit in my life, or in my house, or even on my sofa. What I most regret is not putting a stop to my sister's litany of packages: if I go back over all the boxes she has sent me, it's easy to see that she was preparing me for this last one, the coup de grâce.

I imagine my mother, worried and waiting for me in the apartment. Her nightgown already on, shuffling her flip-flops from here to there. Sometimes, her footsteps sound like the hand that caresses an aching head: 'Sh, sh, sh, it'll be OK.' Other times they are a herd of slithering snakes.

When I get back to the apartment my mother will be a thousand years old, I think.

I will, too. In these past few hours I have aged centuries.

I open the door trying not to make noise. I put the keys in the pocket of my jacket and don't take it off. My bedroom door is open and the bed is made. I tiptoe through the whole apartment and find it empty.

Where haven't I looked?

I have an idea: I go through the kitchen and into the laundry room. The box is assembled, its six panels fitted back together, jammed into the middle of that tiny, damp space. The laundry room doesn't have windows, just some rectangular openings in the wall for ventilation. A faint light filters in and draws stripes of light and shadow on the surface of the box. If it were in a museum, it could be one of those installations that are beautiful in their simplicity, arbitrary in their meaning, and convincing in their evocative spirit.

I make a fist, rap my knuckles against the box a couple of times.

'Mom?'

The silence that follows makes my pulse race.

'Yes?' she answers. 'I'm right here, sweetheart.'

She comes up behind me, from the kitchen, looking at me with some confusion. Her robe, her flip-flops, her thousand years: she's wearing it all.

'What are you doing talking to that box?'

14

I wake up missing Marah.

I remember her lying on the floor of the living room, legs raised to improve circulation, talking to me about the uselessness of practical life and the need to feed one's inner life with sociological theory and those languid books of poetic prose that she likes so much because, she says, she 'prefers literature with no plot', as if such a thing were possible. And sometimes meditation, sometimes vegetables, always psychoanalysis. Choices disguised as a sort of programmatic stripping away, but that, in truth, are mega-capitalist.

Maybe it's not Marah I miss, but being able to talk to someone without the ambition of reaching a conclusion. To blurt out a line of dialogue and follow it to another and another, until one of us gets tired or irritated. Marah is categorical. Her sentences are commandments carved into stone. Her questions and answers – which she usually asks and answers herself – are like slogans: what is civilization? The transformation of raw materials. For the better? Not always. Then for what? To be good for something. When I'm with her, I am also categorical. What saves us, I guess, is that in addition to categorical, we are also useless.

Sometimes I bully her, and she bullies me. Sometimes I think that maybe we care about each other, but deep down we don't like each other much. After our last argument, she left in a huff. It was late, and she said she was going to walk home. She was probably expecting me to invite her to stay over, to remind her that the city is full of rapists. Or else she expected me to invite her to do something that would fix things without making us too vulnerable. We had antidotes. To watch *Friends*, for example. Eight, ten episodes in a row would be enough to turn things around. No more than that; any more would be unbearable. What I did was ask her why she always came to my house, when it was so much uglier than hers. I'd been wanting to ask her that for a long time. Marah was rich, at least by my standards. She lived in a mansion with very high ceilings that was shockingly well-heated. She had a maid she could ask for whatever she wanted, at any hour: from making her a mate – or a Valencian paella – to handing her the pill box where she kept the acid. The night we argued, Marah was sitting on the Chesterfield: knees bent against her chest, chin resting on her knees. And in that pose she stared at the floor, as if she expected someone to whisper the answer to her from down there. I asked if she had any girlfriends besides me.

'Of course I do. Do you?'

I thought of Julia. My first friend when I got to Buenos Aires. She booked shows at a theatre in Boedo. We went out every night and had a great time. I hardly ever saw her during the day. She lived in an old apartment across from a church, and if you looked out from her balcony you saw an imposing dome. One night, at a party at her place, a guy laid her down on the dining room table, which still held plates of leftover food and empty cups, and he took off her shoes and sucked her toes one by one. I was in a chair from where I could see the table from close up, and beyond it the balcony, and beyond that, the dome with the moon to one side.

'I don't think so,' I said.

The thing with the toes didn't shock me in and of itself, but for some reason it made me think back to a couple of nights before: we were closing up the theatre, and Julia asked me to help her pull down the heavy metal shutter, because she was really sore. Why? Because she had got an abortion. 'I didn't think abortions were painful,' I replied quickly. I wanted to keep that space between sentences from filling up with silence. 'Everything that goes through the body hurts,' she had said, with a long-suffering expression that put an end to the conversation.

I could have said something nice. Something that wasn't even an offer of help or a show of solidarity, just something nice. I didn't do it because, when someone reveals that they're unwell, that they're suffering from a burdensome pain, they take on a corporeality that scares me. I understand that we all carry the weight of inhabiting a body, but usually I can forget about it. And when some circumstance outside of my control forces me to imagine a body from inside – the saliva, the blood, inflamed ovaries, intestines packed with decomposed food – my response is to shrink away.

'Why are you my friend?' Marah asked me.

I told her I didn't know. And while I said it I was thinking that Marah wasn't real; nor were our conversations or our fights real, and neither was our friendship. Julia was real, she had a real job, real things happened to her. In her life and in her body. I stopped seeing her because of our schedules, that's what I told her. I should call her some time. But then I would have to explain. Friends like Marah work for me, not friends like Julia.

I can't allow myself the volume taken up by a person afflicted with serious matters, money problems, health issues. I wouldn't know what to do with her. I would end up abandoning her like the plants I didn't plant on my terrace. She would wilt in my hands. There are people – my sister, for example – who have a vocation to maintain relationships, and the more unstable the better: they feel like they can save them. I've seen plenty of people get excited by the idea of being someone else's support; they don't even blink at the needs of others, at illness or grief. It's an arrogant conviction. Those are the same people who later boast about their dedication and demand compensation, but there is nothing in the world that can repay them.

'Well, if you don't have an answer,' said Marah, 'maybe you should reconsider some things…'

My reply was completely hazy, something to buy time. Or silence.

'I guess I need the kind of loyalty that is born of the other person's meanness,' I told her.

'Oh?'

'Yeah, I think that if you were a kind person you wouldn't be my friend. I don't know how to return kindness. Meanness, on the other hand, you get used to.'

She got up with delicate movements, feigning serenity, and put her coat on and left. The next morning she sent me a message: 'A friend is someone who loves you enough to point out your flaws.' Another damned slogan. Then: 'You are lost, but that's not your flaw. Your flaw is that you're a shitty person.'

My mother is already up. I heard her raise the blinds in my room a while ago. They are heavy wooden blinds that make a noise I detest. When blinds are raised – mine, a

134

neighbours' – it means another day has dawned, and that rarely gets me excited. The enthusiasm for doing things like writing, eating, or even bathing and seeing people comes later, after noon.

My phone has six missed calls from Eloy and two from Axel. Axel's are from last night. Eloy's, from very early today.

Late last night, I finished the text on the cow. It's a speech given by the cow itself, talking about its peaceful death. It speaks to the viewer in a voiceover while we see it ambling around a field added in post – the cow, in reality, will be enclosed in a studio with green screens.

I never know if a piece I write is going to work. It depends on the client's whims. It depends on how persuasive Eloy is. On how swollen his face is, I guess.

My job is volatile.

I send a message to Marah. Short and to the point. I wait for the same kind of reply, but it doesn't come.

The blinds in the living room are still down. The little light that enters comes from the hallway to the kitchen and from around the bedroom door. I can see an envelope lying on the floor, which Máximo must have slid under the door last night. It has a cruise ship stamp on it. A card from my sister, I'm sure. I have several that she's sent me over the years from trips she's taken with her family. It's the typical end-of-trip photo that tourism agencies offer: they take it during the first days of vacation, when you've lost your paleness but aren't yet ruined by the sun. You decide how many you want for yourself, and you give them addresses for the people you want to send a copy to. The result is that I often have the picture from her vacation before she does.

I already know what photo that envelope holds: my sister's family in close up, and in the background some Caribbean beach or an infinity pool that looks out over the open sea, blue and brilliant. Her kids and husband must be tanned, in effect, but not my sister. For her, the challenge lies in staying creamy white. She is also flaccid, but that is secondary. Other women judge their sagging bodies to be unsalvageable. I've seen that look, a blend of shame, sadness, and resignation: I am an abandoned village, a no man's land. Not my sister. I never saw anyone so happy with her own body. Every fold, every extra ounce, she accepts it all like a prize for having made it this far. My sister is healthy, curvy, and vivacious. Sure, she goes on diets and does treatments, but she doesn't beat herself up over the results. Quite the contrary, my sister celebrates herself. As long as her skin stays white. And it does: thanks to SPF 100 sunscreens, and hats, parasols, and umbrellas, and a battery of moisturizers. When we were little, we would look at ourselves together in the mirror – to examine ourselves, to find signs of our kinship – and my sister would say: 'We're Ebony and Ivory.' And she felt joy and guilt. The latter didn't last long because, in compensation, she'd say, I was skinny as a post, my hair was 'straight as an Indian's', and, with the right clothes, I had the perfect look to play the typical Hollywood Latina.

The mother tells her daughters stories, but only when they're asleep. She thinks that that way, the stories will stay in the girls' subconscious, which is where things keep the best. It's as if she secretly gave them food to eat that, if they had known, the girls would never have put in their mouths. She tells them legends, likes to teach them about the origins of things. Sometimes she wants to tell them about their own origins, and she says: 'I'm going to tell you our story. It's a beautiful but confused story, because it doesn't have an order, and I don't really know where to begin.' And there she falls silent and tries to organize her ideas, but she can't. 'Why don't I tell you about where whales come from: the sea king lost his wife when she gave birth to her son…'

It's Friday. A week ago at this hour Axel and I were making plans for the evening. We'd decided to see a movie. The theatre was close to my place, so we were going to spend the night here. In the end the movie didn't happen because the theatre was too crowded and scared us away. I don't remember why we didn't end up staying here, though. I do remember a conversation on the terrace about something diffuse that had to do with social media, which neither Axel nor I use. There was a sentence that was left hanging somewhere in the landscape – the branches of the plane tree, Erika's angel trumpet blossoms, the filthy seams of the terrace – because right then we saw the couple across the way leaving with the baby sleeping in its pushchair.

What was that sentence? It had to do with the tendency to build a world populated with like-minded people. And what for? To reinforce one's own opinions and to become radicalized. 'Everyone on their own island, enclosed in their ideology.' Something like that was what Axel said. 'Incapable of… I'm not saying of accepting, or of understanding difference, but of living with it.' He said that, too. I agreed, but I decided to put his reasoning to the test, who knows why. I wondered if closing ourselves off wasn't what everyone had always done, whether they'd had Twitter or not. He and I, for example, would stay together or not depending on our degree of cohesion, or affinity. Any relationship was based on a system of shared beliefs, maybe not identical ones, but similar. Wasn't that what we tried to do? Surround ourselves with padded walls that wouldn't hurt us when we touched them? Get ourselves a good interior, because the outside is threatening? If needles sprouted from the walls we would move away from them, seek the safety of the centre so as not to touch them.

Needles, I think now – that's what my sister and I were for our mother.

And what was she for us? An eclipse.

Maybe, that night last week, the axis that joined Axel and me slipped. Not much, but it led to a smaller rotation. Like when an earthquake happens on one end of the planet and shifts the Earth's position by insignificant degrees that, nonetheless, are enough to shorten days and lengthen nights in the rest of the world. Now it strikes me as pretty clear: while we were watching the couple go out, leaving a wake of lights behind them, our dissent emerged. Axel, faced with my growing mutism (which was not a symptom of disinterest, but rather of reflection), asked me some question that's asked by default when you're getting to know someone. What I mean is, it wasn't an outlandish question. My story, Axel wanted to know my story. My origins. My roots. My reason for being. In my head, I went back over my dense theories about kinship and found them unrepeatable. I found myself looking for simple words to expound on an unproven theory. I abstained; it didn't make sense to drag him into the weeds.

The sound of the shower tends to be intermittent. It changes according to the surface the water is hitting. The tub, an arm, shoulders, head, neck, feet. But in my mother's case I notice that it's invariable, as if the water were always hitting the same rocky surface. I imagine her crouched down, receiving the impact on her back.

I told Axel that I'd tell him 'my story' another day, that I didn't feel like it now. And we stayed there a while longer, gazing out at a view that was the same as before, but didn't seem the same because he'd felt a need to intervene in it, and that was enough to change it.

So that's what it was, then.

Axel, consciously or unconsciously, planted something in my head. His hand grabbed me by the nape of the neck and carried me to face a giant creature that I had decided to ignore, and he made me kneel down in front of it: come on, look at it close, feel the appropriate emotions.

'It's so dark in here.' My mom comes out of the bedroom and opens the blinds in the living room. The light extends over the floor as the blind goes up. I squint to avoid the first full-on blow of sun, a shooting pain in my head. When the blind is about to reach the top, my mom lets go of the cord and covers her mouth with her hands. The dead pigeon is looking in at us, coated in its own blood, dark and dense like a scab.

I run to throw up, but I don't have anything in my stomach.

I get into the shower, turn on the water, and crouch down, letting the water hit me.

My mom is waiting in the living room, ready to go out: trousers, sweater, the shawl wrapped around her. She has a bag in her hand, and inside it is the pigeon. We leave. The hallway is freezing, and so is the elevator. It's strange not to run into anyone at this time of the morning. It's strange that a woman who claims to be my mother is taking me by the elbow and directing my steps.

Downstairs, my mom throws the bag into the container across the street. She takes my elbow again and we walk. The breeze on my face does me good. I'm dizzy from lack of food. Before we turn the corner I look back to see if Máximo has come out to sweep, or if there's anyone on the front steps. No one. The block is empty and carpeted with brown leaves.

'Where are we going?' I ask her when we've been walking for several blocks and she shows no sign of stopping.

'There.' She points straight ahead, towards the building under construction that we can see from my balcony. 'I want to see it from close up.'

I look at her profile. The roots of her hair are white. There are wrinkles I hadn't seen before in her delicate skin. I'm walking beside my own future.

The building is locked up, as always. Yellow tape hugs its perimeter. The windows, lined inside with dark paper, show my reflection, and when I see myself there I think of the continuity of other people's bodies in mine. I see my mother's features cast in my face, and my grandmother's sharp chin, and that little mark at the end of one eyebrow that could be a scar, except that my sister has it too. A mysterious mark that has neither origin nor story. When I asked my sister where that twin scar came from, she shook her head: 'I don't know anything about it.' The wind turns colder. I look up towards the roof of the unfinished building, thinking how much I like it. It reminds me of the size of human ambition. And of madness. Like going into a Renaissance building and looking at the ceiling to feel our smallness. I imagine that if the building were to collapse and crush me, some part of all the people who inhabit me would die, too. When someone ceases to exist they take a piece of you with them, a material, concrete piece, not just a collection of memories. And when someone is born they debut old features, they come with a burden of past that will always be bigger than their future. That's what it means to procreate: to break off a piece of your matter and history and offer it to the world so it doesn't rot along with you. The refusal to be extinguished. The effort to endure. A stingy and narcissistic desire. There are many days when my desire is for the wind to carry me off like dust. To disappear. That's what I've been doing, anyway. Distancing myself, dissolving. The very few times I've run into people from my past – from my childhood, my adolescence, from my city – I could see the surprise in their eyes, hear it in their tone of voice, as if they were looking at a ghost: 'You disappeared,' they say, though it's obvious I didn't, that I'm right here, trapped in the same package as always. The expression on their faces is never pleasant, as if knowing I was far away had given them the certainty that I was OK, but now, seeing me again, they can't help but think that something went wrong. A return, almost always, is a failure.

There are days when I want to disappear after a final sigh of exhaustion. But the relief vanishes when I think I will have passed through the world with nothing to hold onto. Who could I leave a message for, a surrender, an apology? Who would put me on trial?

15

'Remember how we were going to put in a pool?'

'But it would have taken up too much of the yard.'

'I would've liked a pool.'

'Well, sorry.'

'Whatever happened to Eusebio?'

'…you did have an infinite ocean just down the hill.'

'Full of dying creatures.'

'That was because of the seaweed, it was poisonous.'

'It's weird that you don't know anything about Eusebio and Machi.'

'Machi, I do, she was with me until she died.'

'Machi's dead?'

'Choked on a bone, can you believe it?'

'Christ.'

'Like a dog.'

'Did Machi have any kids?'

'About a thousand.'

'Where are they?'

'I have no idea, honey.'

The night is a locked box. For two hours now I haven't been able to get to my feet. Dinner disagreed with me. Everything makes me sick. My body is acting very strangely these days. Maybe my stomach isn't used to that food anymore. My mom and I are on the terrace; we're surrounded by an invisible capsule of thick walls that muffles the sound from the street and transforms it into an aggravating whisper. I think: this is a dream or a hangover. I'm cold. There's a blanket over my shoulders and another on my lap. My mother just has the shawl: it falls solemnly, like the cloak of a goddess. If I don't move, the discomfort subsides. I use the blanket on my shoulders to improvise a pillow against the backrest and lean my head on it. Not a single star. The same deep, cornerless sky. From this very chair, I've already watched several summers die as cold, grey autumns are born.

'The lamp in the living room is broken, sweetheart.'

'I know.'

My mother's house didn't have much furniture. Some parts of the concrete floor had been pushed up by roots that ran underneath, and some corners had creeping plants climbing up the wall. Everything creaked. The damp made the wood swell and shrink. My aunt said that houses were like women: when they got married they were pretty and clean, but then they were used, kids came along and ruined them, got them dirty, wore them out, and there was no going back.

That is: inaugurating a body or a house is to commence its deterioration.

Deterioration, I think now, is a superior state of matter because it means something has flourished in it. Only that which has given fruit can rot.

That house held echoes: of wind shaking the trees, of rain hitting the windows, of someone crying in a bathroom, of the fox in the attic. Twice, we tried to poison the fox, and twice it didn't work. It ate the raw meat we left out, licked the plate clean, but it didn't die. Maybe the poison had expired. One of those times, Eusebio went up through the hatch into the attic and found it with its nose in the dish: he carefully reached out his arms, and when he was good and close he grabbed it around the neck and picked it up. The fox shrieked and struggled so hard that Eusebio fell down the steps still holding on to the animal. The fox fell on its belly so hard it vomited blood. We thought something inside had burst. But when Eusabio let it go, thinking he'd won, the fox pounced on him and scratched his face, leaving some raw wounds that hurt to look at. Then it ran back up the steps and jumped through the hatch into the attic.

'You never learned to kill animals?' I ask my mom.

She doesn't answer. I don't insist, just close my eyes.

After dinner, my mother convinced me to take three tablespoons of passionflower tincture. 'You'll see, it switches you off,' she told me.

Before dinner, I'd got a message from the building chat: Carla was calling a meeting for tomorrow morning. It was very unusual to meet on a Saturday. That's how mad Erika must be. The subject said: '7B, Various.'

I also got a message from Marah: she would try to come by tomorrow night.

I want to prepare our encounter. I want to abstain from fighting. I plan to make it through by carrying out small tasks: put the kettle on, peel oranges, listen to her without interrupting. Listening is a sign of hospitality: I'll cede the available air in my house so your words can circulate. Meanwhile, I'll do things. Doing things is easy. When you do things that way, without thinking, you don't need answers, just reactions. Mate? Yes. Sugar? Sure. Sofa or terrace? Terrace. It's scary how many things can be done without thinking. Eat, drink, kill, live.

Other people solve their problems by pushing the ends towards the middle to try and eliminate the gap of incomprehension. There, in the middle, they set up two chairs and settle in for a chat. Really, it's more of a 'dialogue'. But the gap never closes completely, there's always air there, a small but expandable fissure. Every person is a nucleus bordered by gaps of incomprehension. Even those who sit the closest are separated by that thin but deep edge. No one is that close to anyone. No one can obviate the abyss that isolates them from everyone else.

Marah and I ignore the abyss, we pretend not to see it, and sometimes it works. Other times, one of us drags the other up to a dangerous edge where we not only see the void, we also feel the vertigo.

'Go on to bed.' My mother's hand on my shoulder feels huge and heavy. I open my eyes slowly. I see her face too close to mine.

Axel hasn't called me all day.

'Have you seen the cat today?' I ask as I get up from my chair with the motor skills of an old lady. She doesn't answer, or I don't hear her.

In the afternoon I left a bowl of food out for Catrina. I put it right here on the terrace, but I don't see it now. I didn't have cat food so I gave her scraps. I thought that if I gave her more food, she would stop bringing me cadavers.

'I'm not scared,' I say, I don't know why.

Because of the passionflower.

My mother takes me by the arm and leads me to the bedroom.

'Should I be scared?'

'No, no, none of that,' she says, patting my back.

'Are you going to tell me what you came here to tell me?'

'Of course I am.'

'When?'

'It's a beautiful story.'

'But when?'

'Though it's a little confused.'

'Because…?'

'But deep down it's very simple.

'Deep down where?'

She helps me sit on the bed. I lay my head on the pillow and hear her flip-flops shuffle away. She turns out the light, leaves the room, closes the door, and leaves a hole in the air. I put my hands beside my eyes to restrict my vision more, to keep from getting distracted. Like an ox pulling a plough. When the field is too wide, I have trouble distinguishing the essential from the incidental. That's why I'm like this, I think, because I grew up looking at the horizon. Rambling, daydreaming, escaping. I need to impose a frame on myself. I need to try out a new awareness. At least for tonight, to concentrate on what I can see before my eyes. The jungle of banana trees, the poisonous seaweed, my mother's shoes lying in the dirt like two dead birds.

Half-sleep is deceitful. Lying in my bed with my eyes closed, it seems like it's been months since the last time Axel came to my house. Before his whales, before that convoluted conversation on the terrace, before the dissent, we were together on my sofa. It was a crossing of the threshold, two steps taken, and a fall onto that soft and slightly lumpy surface – I presume its ex-owner, the dead old lady, put it to good use before I did.

I remember Axel's body on top of mine, pressing just enough to impede movement without suffocating me. Axel is good with his hands. They're well-trained, it's obvious. How many pairs of trousers has he had to unbutton and lower in order to learn how to fit perfectly between a girl's legs without taking off all her clothes? While I was under there, breathing the scarce air between his chest and my face, overcome by blind hedonism, I thought that such intensity might be capable of dislocating me. An electrical charge, that's what happened. My mouth, with every exhale, blew puffs of smoke.

Still with my eyes closed, I got into a car with Axel and we took off down a straight, continuous highway. He was driving and I was looking out the window at the view – flat land, green and empty – and every once in a while I turned towards him as he focused on the road, one arm resting on the window, the sleeve of his shirt flapping frantically.

When pleasure melts, it leaves a puddle of melancholy.

Then came silence. We stayed there in that narrow space, his pale arm pressed against my brown one in a stark – and ad-worthy – contrast. The only light came from outside, and each shade grew extreme in the presence of the other, as if they needed affirmation. Intimacy between two people is made of these silences, I thought. There are other things made of silence: trust, perfumes, literature. I like silence, but it loses its charm when it's practised by one person. Between two, on the other hand, it signifies fullness. It also means the illusion of permanence. But it's unreliable; sometimes silence is just a way of hiding fragility, of looking at each other to corroborate a happiness sullied by the fear that if someone were to mention it aloud, it would break.

16

It's so cold I don't want to move. It's the cold of a house that has been empty for a long time. I realize that if I slept in my bed, my mother must have slept on the sofa, and I feel anxious and ashamed. I jump out of bed and open the blinds in my room. The morning sun hurts, even this depressed sun. Before leaving the room I go to the bathroom and sit down to pee; I need to shower to really wake up. Yesterday was a stressful day, I think as I get undressed. Seen in the light of a new day, it was completely ridiculous. What exactly can they accuse me of at this meeting? Throwing dead animals on the neighbour's terrace? It's not true, but suppose I admit guilt just to cut my losses. OK, I'm sorry, it was an accident, I won't get into details. Case closed. What else can the word 'various' encompass?

The messages in the building chat are euphemistic and grandiloquent. The neighbours think of themselves as a group of people who have been tasked with a transcendent mission. To take care of the property, to protect those bricks that, of course, matter more than the people who inhabit them. It's utterly logical, and there's even some justice in it: the bricks will endure. Many of us who attend those meetings aren't even owners. It doesn't matter, they're mandatory. We have to be informed of collective decisions, and the distinction between collective and personal is always diffuse. Whether this neighbour can have a party on Thursday; whether this wall can be torn down to make a room bigger, and during what hours. I think of Erika and Tomás's apartment. They tore down walls and more walls until they created not space, but emptiness. They needed to create that emptiness so they could then fill it with sober tastes straight out of a magazine, and feel themselves to be masters. In the end, that's what it's all about: tear down, sweep up the dust, re-inhabit, take possession.

I get out of the shower, wrap a towel around myself, and go to the bedroom. My hair is dripping onto the floor, so I wrap it in the towel instead. I look at myself naked in the mirror on the inside of the closet door. I don't know what to think about my body, except that it's still young; does that mean it's pretty? Is young the same thing as pretty? According to whom? I should have a more well-defined opinion of my own body: like my sister, like Axel, like León's ex-babysitter. I don't hear anything from outside. I'm hungry. I get my phone from the bedside table: twenty to eleven. I put on jeans, a white t-shirt, black hoodie, ankle boots. I rub my hair with the towel and blow it dry, then look at myself again in the mirror. I look good, the sleep has healed me. I put on an imperceptible pink lipstick, and it reflects onto my cheeks. It's good not to look unkempt, but it's no good to show off. The lipstick has the colour of health: I look fresh, not made up.

My mother is not on the sofa or in the kitchen. Nor on the terrace. I sigh. This damned maniacal game.

'Mom?'

No answer.

I open the fridge; there's hardly anything left. Eight days ago it looked like a wartime bunker, and today I'm a charity case. Maybe my mom went down to the store for provisions. It would be strange, but it's possible. I picture her with the shopping bag, walking indecisively from here to there, trying to find the corner store that I point out every time we leave: if you need something, come here; if you need money, there's some in the kitchen drawer, beside the keys, with the notepad.

I pour a glass of milk and drink it.

My sister's card is still in its envelope on the counter. I see that underneath it is another envelope and a box of coconut candies I hadn't seen. I open the card first: it's the photo I was expecting. My sister and her family in white clothes beside an open sea, so blue it looks like they used a filter. The other envelope doesn't have any writing on it. I open it and find a photo with a yellow Post-it note stuck on it: 'Surprise', it says in my sister's handwriting. I pull off the Post-it: it's the two of us sitting on a tree trunk at my mother's house. I don't remember this moment. How old was I? Six, seven? Who took that picture? Maybe my sister doesn't know either, because neither of us is looking into the camera. She seems to be talking to me. Maybe she's telling me one of her family stories in which we all die at some point, poisoned or drowned or gutted like pigs by the road. The back of the photo doesn't have a date, but there's a note written in handwriting I don't recognize: 'Look, they're like bottles. Choose one or two things (not five, not ten, not a thousand) to put inside them, in their heads. They should be things that can travel a long way without going bad. Then toss them out to sea, let them go.' I read the note several times, and check the envelope in case there's something else, but there's nothing. I get nervous, and I want to call my sister so she can explain this new old photo. Who wrote that note? What does it mean? As I read it, it seems like there was a plan for us. Or that day, at least, someone believed there should be a plan, and they gave a series of instructions. What happened, then? Did the plan fail? Did the plan work? Was this the plan? I want to wait for my mom and show her the picture, but it's already nearly eleven. I open the box of candy and eat one hurriedly, then another, then run to brush my teeth. I throw on a scarf and jacket and go out into the hallway, which is freezing. I take a deep breath and press the elevator button.

While I go down I picture the hall as Máximo has arranged it: the plastic chairs in a semi-circle; to one side, the table where they put the thermos of water and the mate, which circulates hand to hand in simulated tribal ritual. I can't get used to the practice of sharing mate between strangers. 'Don't you like it?' they ask and look at me in surprise as if they were before an indecipherable enigma. The surprise means they attribute universality to a personal habit, and that they have contempt for things that seem foreign, distant, unknown. No one ever asked what I did drink; maybe not to offer me some, but to at least make room for me in that homogenous group, so I wouldn't be the only one who didn't drink mate, but just the girl who prefers tea. I shake my head shyly at the question: 'No, I don't like it.' And to top it off, I apologize: 'I'm sorry.' But it's a lie. I do like mate. I love it. I drink mate all day long. But I'd rather lie so as not to isolate myself even more with the violent confession that their orgy of slobber makes me sick.

°

I sit down in one of the empty chairs. I want to check the time and pat my pockets, looking for my phone. I left it upstairs. The elevator opens and I see Susan come out leading León by the hand. She apologizes: she didn't have anyone to leave the kid with. She sits down and hands León her phone to play with. He takes it with a smile and goes to sit in a corner, his back against the wall and legs out in front of him.

We are all seated, except Máximo; he stands leaning against the doorway of his security booth, which is small and unclean. I've never seen him inside the booth. During working hours he sweeps, and the rest of the time he hides away in his ground floor apartment.

I see the man who always prepares the mate, but there's no mate today.

Carla is about to start the session: she rises from her chair and clears her throat. Carla is long, sharp, and serious as a military sword.

'We all know why we're here,' she says.

All of us? I look around to see if anyone shares my confusion. No one.

'I don't know,' I say.

'Well,' says Carla, 'the subject of the meeting said "Various 7B". So, we're going to talk about your apartment.'

'Oh, OK. Since it said "various", I thought maybe there were more than one.'

No one laughs. Sometimes I feel obliged to act the fool, to be childish in order to offset the darkness. Something dark is coming, you can feel it in the air. In the ever more severe expressions. Erika and Tomás are at one end of the semi-circle, holding hands. Carla turns to them:

'Erika, do you want to start?'

Erika nods. She says that several days ago she started to notice strange things going on in my apartment.

'Strange things,' I repeat. Or ask. It's unclear.

'Dear,' says Carla, sitting now, 'you can't interrupt.'

I don't want to interrupt, I want to smash everything.

'Sorry,' I reply. 'But when you put it like that it could mean anything from a satanic cult to organ trafficking.'

'This isn't funny,' says Erika. Her mouth is a grimace of disgust, as if she'd spent years imitating the expression of someone who needs to throw up.

'I'm not saying it's funny, just unspecific. You can't throw out sentences that are all fizzy and expect a concrete answer, Erika.'

It must be the first time I've called her by her name.

'...The choice to use the expression "strange things" over so many others you could use has to come with a cost. Why? There's certainly a high cost for the rest of us.'

Some of my neighbours are giving me strange looks, and seem impatient or distracted. When I get angry I lose the thread of what I'm saying, I talk just to talk and others get confused by my words. But it's not my strategy to confuse them, it's not intentional. It's just nervous awkwardness.

'Let her talk, please,' interrupts Carla, the mistress of ceremonies.

In any case, the blame for their lack of understanding is not mine alone. No one takes the time necessary to comprehend an idea that's half-formed, sure, but has enough clues that if someone wanted to understand, they could. And that reaction is not so far removed from indifference.

'We all want this to be over soon,' says Carla.

Or contempt.

'Right?' she insists, looking at me.

I wave a hand as though saying, do what you want, I couldn't care less. I look towards the exit, mulling the idea of an escape. My mother is out there, and she could come back any minute. I picture her bursting into the room like a lightning bolt that splits the sky and illuminates the night. This would be a good time to introduce her to the neighbours. A mother, in a narrow values system, generates respect, compassion, empathy. It does people good to see that they're not alone in this – the business of having a mother.

After gulping air as if she were about to dive into a swamp, Erika starts up again: she talks about the dead rat, the dead pigeon, and she adds that the downstairs neighbours (I don't know which of the people in the semi-circle they are) complained that I dumped my dustpan onto their balcony, which I had also done on her terrace. She mentions the incident on Thursday: I, an adult and presumably sane woman, jumped the dividing wall over to her side, and spied on her through the window. She shakes her head:

'We're not used to living like this.'

There's a general murmur, a unanimous agreement with her testimony.

Where is my mother?

'Do you have anything to say, dear?' Carla asks. Her tone is an attempt at tolerance, but her meanness gets in the way.

'It's all lies,' I say. 'It's nonsense. The cat goes out and brings dead animals back. It's the cat, not me, and it's all so ridiculous. On Thursday I jumped over to their terrace to get the dead pigeon that the cat left there, not to spy on them…'

No one says anything.

'Yesterday, the dead pigeon was on my terrace again.' I look at Erika, who is typing on her phone. 'Who put it there, Erika?'

She doesn't react. It's as if a crazy person were talking. Now I look at Susan.

155

'Susan, can you tell them, please?' I say.

Susan is caught off-guard.

'Tell them what?'

'That you saw the cat in my house the other night.'

'Yes, yes, I did see her.'

'And León saw her with the dead pigeon in her mouth.' I turn to León, who is engrossed in a game on the phone. He's moving his thumbs anxiously, as though squashing bugs. 'Right, León?'

León doesn't look up, so I insist.

'Hey, León.'

The boy looks at me without understanding why I'm interrupting his trance.

'Let's leave the child out of this,' says Carla, giver of justice.

'But he did see her,' I insist.

León has already returned to the screen. His mother is looking at the floor. Erika leans her head against Tomás's shoulder; he is red and mortified.

'All right,' says Carla. 'Let's suppose it was the cat.'

'Let's suppose?' I want to shout.

'We still have another little problem.'

'Oh, do we?' I get up from the chair because I feel unbearably hot. The pit of my stomach is burning.

Carla sighs and looks at Máximo, who has been silent, unable to hide his satisfaction. Máximo hates me more than the others, because he can't accept that someone like me is 'above' someone like him. He can bow and cringe like a golem before anyone else present here, but his blood boils at having to take out the garbage of a foreign upstart with an Indian face and airs of superiority.

Máximo pulls some plastic gloves from his trouser pocket and puts them on. He goes into his booth and comes back out, his bearing that of a prehistoric creature emerging from a cave. He's carrying a black bag, which he holds out so everyone can see it, and in a single movement he extracts the stiff body of Catrina. He holds her by the feet and lifts her up like an irrefutable fact. León bursts out crying, and Susan runs to him. I drop into my chair. I can hear distant, indistinguishable murmurs. A noise of hot voices that burn and grate. Catrina's eyes are two dry, motionless stones.

17

It's Saturday, and there's almost no one in the park. It's a miracle. I've been here nearly two hours, I guess: I don't have my phone to check. A while ago, I realized that the spider mural isn't really a spider – it's missing two legs. Maybe it's a wounded spider. The bug on the mural, in any case, has six legs, and its body is formed by a lot of dots with no outline.

I sat down to listen to the birds. I remembered León from two days ago as he ran around a tree: 'I'm an invisible ninja warrior.' I fell asleep, then woke up gasping for air. Something similar had happened to me at the building meeting – I felt strangled by the pressure of all those eyes looking from Catrina to me, from me to Catrina, as if they were expecting some kind of transmutation. I leapt from my chair as soon as I was capable and fled outside without waiting for a verdict. I walked until I got my breath back and ended up here. I cried. A woman gave me a pack of disposable tissues. 'Are you OK?' she asked. I nodded. After a while I stood up and took a few laps around the park on its curved walkway made of grey slabs that shine in the sun, when there's sun. But the sun isn't out today, and the slabs look like gravestones.

'Got a smoke?' I hear from behind me. It's the same man as always. I curse him silently. I turn around and tell him I don't have one. He smiles at me: a line of yellow teeth stuck into dark, swollen gums. His eyes are small, their blue faded. He takes a step forward; he smells sour. He stretches his arms out wide like a hawk spreading its wings; he feints a lunge at me with a quick movement that startles me. I recoil instinctively and try to turn around to run away, but my feet get tangled up and I fall. Face against ground, nose smashed, blood flowing like a tap that's been turned on. The guy takes off, laughing and walking aimlessly.

I get to my feet and hurry out of the park. On the way to the building I see Susan coming towards me.

'I found you!' she says, crossing the street at a trot. When she's closer, she scrunches up her face in an expression of pain. 'Ouch. What happened?'

'I fell.'

Susan takes my face in her hand, examines my nose and says it's nothing, just some broken vessels, that's why there's so much blood.

'It bleeds like this sometimes anyway,' I tell her.

'It's going to turn purple, or green, or both.'

'I know.'

She takes my arm and walks with me, saying she can patch me up.

In her apartment she takes out a first aid kit, wets some cotton with iodine, and cleans me up. Then come the Band-Aids, the delicate work of her nurse's hands. She finishes and inspects me.

'Like new.'

I ask her why she'd been looking for me before.

'Well, you took off so fast and I wanted to follow you, but I couldn't catch you. We went upstairs because León was really shocked by the cat, he couldn't stop crying.'

She shakes her head, holding back tears of her own. 'You have to be a real garbage heap of a person to put a little animal on display like that, like a useless slab of meat.'

Once he calmed down, León told her to look for me in the park. It took her a while to make the whole round until she found me.

'I see.'

I'm hungry. I ask Susan if she has anything to eat. The glass of milk and the coconut candies are the only thing I have in my stomach, and this burning sensation won't go away. She brings me some toast, apple juice, and an aspirin.

'I wanted to tell you that I don't care what those people down there said about you, I know you're a good person.'

I don't answer. I don't even know myself whether I'm a good person.

'If I were you, I'd file a complaint…' Susan goes on.

It's surprising how other people will urge you to do things they wouldn't even dream of doing themselves. Susan wouldn't file a complaint about anyone, because she is a coward. I could have used her support when the neighbours were all piling on me, but she thought it was more interesting to stare at the granite tile of the stairway. Being good and supportive under ordinary circumstances isn't worth anything, Susan, it's like turning on a flashlight in the middle of the day.

I scarf down the toast and ask for more juice. The burning subsides a little.

Susan comes back with the full glass and hands it to me.

'Do you have a boyfriend?' she asks.

'What?'

'Sorry. Occupational hazard, I guess. But you're looking pretty pale and that appetite is suspicious.' She laughs with a mischievousness that doesn't match my mood.

'Oh?'

'You don't think you could be pregnant?'

I feel the air drive into my chest. I stand up, leaving the juice untouched on the table. I tell her I'm tired, and I want to go home.

'I'm sorry, I didn't mean to be nosy.'

'No, don't worry about it.'

I go out to the hallway and press the elevator button.

A continuous buzzing starts in my ears. It's the sound that's left by a firecracker. Or after something huge falls from the roof: you don't see it coming until the floor shakes and cracks.

My mother is still missing.

I get my laptop and sit on the sofa to open the grant file. I read part of what I've written:

The mother and her two daughters live together in a house, but they don't see each other. They communicate through a notepad on the kitchen table. The notes are almost always about practical matters: food, shopping, household chores, the inclement weather. The weather where they live is inclement every day: there is a sun that burns like fire, and rain falls in the form of devastating storms that knock over trees and enrage the sea. The older girl is in charge of writing the notes for their mother. If the milk runs out, the older girl opens the notepad, writes the date, and then: Buy milk. Or: We need new sandals. Or: We can't sleep because of the fox. The mother crosses things out as she resolves them, and she occasionally writes notes too: Go down to the beach, but wear shoes, it's covered with pink corals that are beautiful but sharp. Or: I picked some mangos for you, they're ripe and sweet. Or: Do you two really think that chicken feet are garbage? The younger girl doesn't write much, she prefers to look for her mother around the house, though she never finds her. She follows in her footsteps, which are silent but leave a black, melted mark wherever she goes. The floor of the house is full of these marks, which draw circular labyrinths. Sometimes she also hears the mother's voice giving instructions to the caretaker, and she runs to where she thinks she'll find her, but doesn't get there in time. Though she still can't write well, she also leaves some notes in the book. She writes the date: Today. And then she writes: Where are you? The next day she finds the answer. Ha! What a crazy question! I'm right here, child, don't you see me?

I think: I have something to say, but I don't know how to say it.

I think: Is that how my mother feels too?

I think: This novel has too many animals.

I close the laptop; I'm tired. I want to sleep and wake up someplace else. I want to sleep and wake up in another body. I go to the bathroom, find the bottle of passionflower tincture, and take the rest of it.

What if I renounced everything? What is everything? Axel, my job, the grant, my sister, Marah. Oh God, Marah. The idea of seeing her today stresses me out. I imagine texting her to cancel. 'I don't feel good, let's reschedule.' She'd respond immediately: 'Everything has its limit.' And me: 'If everything is Everything, it can't have a limit, that doesn't make sense.' She'd send me a gif that says 'Fuck you.'

I can't cancel. I can't burn all my bridges.

My eyes are closing, and I lower the blinds.

I call the pharmacy and order a pregnancy test.

At around six I wake up and call Eloy:

'I was about to call Childline and report you missing,' he says.

'I had some awful problems in my building.'

'What kind of problems?'

'Nothing important, shitty neighbours.'

'Like all neighbours.'

'What do I know.'

'Are they kicking you out?'

'Are *you* kicking me out?'

He laughs. I hear the sound of ice in a glass, and then a long sigh.

'Not today.'

He tells me that they didn't approve the cow campaign. That is, they cancelled it. It had already been approved; in fact, they'd paid in advance for the first pieces. And now it was all going into the garbage.

'No, please, it wasn't because of your copy.' His tone makes it clear that the mere thought that I was at fault is to give myself too much importance.

They never even read my piece.

Eloy had liked it. A little metaphysical, maybe, but anyway, it really didn't matter now. Metaphysical? What are you talking about, *Horacio*?

'I mean there's no more campaign,' he repeats.

'But, why?' I ask.

He says they haven't got a certification they need in order to launch the brand. According to the client, the slaughterhouses lobbied against them, 'some shit like that'. But Eloy doesn't believe the client. He thinks they went to another agency; he'll find out.

'I see.'

'It was a lot of money,' I hear him swallow.

'I'm sorry,' I say.

'It's all good.'

Where is Eloy's son?

a) With his mother and her boyfriend, a well-intentioned guy who has no idea how to talk to a child.

b) At the movies with his best friend's family: for now they seem loving and affectionate, but in a few years he will hate them because they represent everything he doesn't have (he won't put it like this to himself, of course. He'll think: 'Their hypocrisy is disgusting.')

c) Locked in a room playing video games. Angry at the world but safe.

'See you Monday?' I ask him.

'Did you know that in some parts of the world, they masturbate pigs before killing them?'

'Oh?'

'It's to get rid of their stress. So they're relaxed when they die.'

'Did you suggest the client use that method on their cows?'

'No, but I could. I mean, if what they're worried about is a violent and painful death... But what do I know about how to masturbate a cow.'

'Pigs, though, you're an expert on.'

This time his laughter is thunderous. He's drunk. I wonder if I should hang up or if I have a duty to listen to him. Not for my job, but out of pity.

'No one used to think about how animals died, you know? Now they're obsessed with not letting them suffer, but it's inconsistent with the fact that, once they're dead, people still eat them, don't you think?'

Eloy needs to talk. The subject is secondary, as is the interlocutor. He just wants to be listened to and receive supportive words in reply.

'And thus a vegan is born,' I say.

Talking, for some people, is a way to alleviate their misery.

'I'm not a big fan of animals,' he says. Some people knit, Eloy talks. 'But I don't like people that much, either.'

I don't answer. My nap knocked me out. It was long and out of the ordinary. I had weird dreams.

'Are you there?' Eloy asks.

'Yeah, I'm just tired.'

I hear ice in the glass again.

I dreamed about my father, but I don't remember what happened. Everything I know about my dad is in that photo my sister keeps in her closet. A well-groomed man, thick-rimmed glasses and plaid shirt. His eyes were big and black, his expression happy. A happy man. It could be the generic picture in a frame bought at the pharmacy. 'That's because you didn't know him,' my sister replied when I told her he had a blank face. She *had* known him: during her first five years, but to me that doesn't seem like enough, either. Enough for what? To feel a belonging. And how long *is* enough?

'OK,' says Eloy. 'Thanks for listening.'

'No problem.'

'Get some rest, kiddo.'

We hang up.

I will never feel a belonging. It doesn't matter how much I force the thread of kinship and memory to find the meaning, the origin, the seed of belonging. Unless the seed of belonging is not buried, like a fossil, in the past. I think that if the present is saturated by the past, if it already contains the past and can't get rid of it – because getting rid of it would be to get rid of the present itself – it is also useless to search in the here and now. The past and the present are hiding places I already know, even if I still don't understand them, even though I try so hard to understand them, as if understanding were really such a great thing. Wanting to understand is ambitious; it would be enough, maybe, to be able to tell them apart. What was before, what is now, where does everything begin and end. I don't have the patience to organize a timeline. The succession of scenes gets mixed up in my head and I still can't find what I'm after.

I rule out the past and I rule out the present. I should look somewhere else.

Where haven't I looked?

I sit on the sofa to wait for Axel. I am also waiting for my mother. Or so I think. I'm also waiting for Marah, though she might not show up. Maybe Axel won't, either. I texted him saying I wanted to talk and he said: 'I'll stop by later.' Imprecise and discouraging. I sent him a whale emoji, then a gun. He sent me the crying with laughter face and a heart with an arrow through it. That made me feel better. And my relief led to the thought that placing my trust in juvenile emojis is not very intelligent of me.

It looks like rain.

Maybe no one will come and I will wait forever.

I'm hit by a more extreme suspicion: maybe I have never moved from this spot. I've been planted right here for ages. I am both bloom and extinction. There is nothing in between.

I go to the kitchen. In the pantry, an open bag of tortilla chips survives. The fridge holds water, cookies on a plate, and a jar of olives with no olives, only brine. My paltry reserves. I open the drawer where I keep the notepad. It doesn't have many notes; some household reminders to myself, and an old message Marah left one time when she slept over and left before I woke up – 'Buy food!' I turn to a blank page and write: 'Where are you?'

There is no light in the living room, everything is in shadow.

I go out to the terrace. I press on my eyes until white spots emerge like drops on the black background and spread out until they consume it. I have the idea that when I remove my hands and open my eyes I'll find that the world has returned to its basic shape from eight days ago. Back when the worms in my head were still active, prolific, controlled. Right now they are still. Asleep. Maybe broken. Doesn't matter. Some worms can split into segments that survive.

I have a plan: I'll take the test when someone gets here. The first one to arrive will witness how this plastic object, which looks like an unsophisticated thermometer, transforms into evidence of a future. Or not.

First I showered, dried my hair, looked at myself in the mirror and saw that the bruise was still there: between my nose and left cheek, darker and more swollen. I put on trousers with an elastic waist and no zipper that will make my task easier. I put on the 'Rabid Fox' sweatshirt.

The plane tree's dry leaves are still falling. Catrina could hear the sound they made when they hit the sidewalk. A very soft crack that made her prick up her ears and open her eyes wide. Her senses sharpened before the inevitable.

The apartment of the couple and their baby is still illuminated and empty, like one who doesn't lose faith.

I look for the intangible connection between my mother and my child, if it is true that something is throbbing inside me: a tiny heart floating like a dumpling.

I go back to the sofa, lie down holding the box with the test, and close my eyes. To distract myself, I think about movies. All the ones I can remember are about the same thing: loss. And waiting. I think of E.T., abandoned by his ship – that is, by his mother – on a hostile planet, in

168

a house without a father or any rules about eating healthy or dressing well. I think about Giovanni Sermonti, about Molly Jensen, Antoine Doniel, Maggie Fitzgerald, Arthur Fleck, Ally Campana, about Maleficent. They've all lost something, they're all waiting for something to repair them or for their segments to survive.

I imagine my mother comes in and says: You're about to become someone's home. I ask: What did you do to Catrina? There is no answer.

I imagine Marah comes in and tells me that it's the opposite. What is the opposite? Of what your mom said. She says: Someone is about to become *your* home. I ask: How many pesos is five hundred pounds?

I imagine my sister comes in: Congratulations, she says, only that which has borne fruit can rot.

The door buzzer sounds. I get up to answer.

I make quick calculations: it would be born in summer, right when the heat begins. I like the summer. Life explodes in shades of green.

Director & Editor: Carolina Orloff
Director: Samuel McDowell

www.charcopress.com

The Delivery was published on
80gsm Munken Premium Cream paper.

The text was designed using Bembo 11.5 and ITC Galliard.

Printed in June 2023 by TJ Books
Padstow, Cornwall, PL28 8RW using responsibly
sourced paper and environmentally-friendly adhesive.